Karaoke Chemistry

VALERIE PEPPER

Cover Design: Lyssa at Booked Forever Shop

Editor: Katie at Spice Me Up Editing

Published by Stafford Lane Publishing, LLC

For my sister, Emily

Magnolia

PULLING INTO A partially hidden space, I kill the engine and reach into the back seat for my canvas tote. It's a familiar routine at this point, throwing on the black tee with a glitter skull over my pink tank top and wiggling into ripped black jeans. I slide off the muted cotton skirt and open my makeup kit to line my eyes in the visor mirror with a royal blue glitter eyeliner, then smudge it. After fluffing up my limp hair, I get out and step to the back of my Fiat to shove my feet into the black Doc Martens that are only worn here. I lock my car, hustle to the door, then take a deep breath. I always expect a tingle of magic to course through me before I step inside, but it never happens. And since it's magic's fault that I'm even in this position, you'd think it would have the decency to show up.

It doesn't.

It never does.

Which is for the best. It's why I'm here, after all.

Wrenching the door open, I step into the dimly-lit bar. The familiar scents of old wood and alcohol wrap around me as I head straight for Carol, weaving through the crowd of people I make a point never to speak with and past the bar. I find her bent over tonight's list, and she straightens as I near, smiling in delight. "Seven! I didn't think you'd make it tonight."

I start to apologize, but Seven doesn't say sorry. Ever. So I stand tall and shrug like it's no big deal. "Hi, Carol. Had some things to do today. You know how it goes."

She hands me the pen and my silver bracelets clink against each other as I write my name and song selections down. It's been a *day,* so I choose Joan Jett's "I Love Rock 'n' Roll" and No Doubt's "Just a Girl," two fun songs that I can easily lose myself in and forget the rest of the world. I'm last on the list, but Carol likes me—or at least the twenties I give her every time I sing—so I know I'll get on stage tonight.

I hand the pen back with a smile and make my way to the bar to order Seven's usual drink: a high-end whiskey, neat, water on the side. When I'm at Al's, I'm not Magnolia Rowan, quiet high school chemistry teacher and least interesting of the many Rowan sisters. Here, I'm Seven, bad-ass singer who doesn't care what anyone thinks. Who can't harm anyone with her voice. I can flirt with the bartender even though he looks like he's barely old enough to drink, let alone serve alcohol. It's only here that I'm a woman who takes what she wants. Who is unapologetically herself. Who has a powerhouse voice, literally *and* metaphorically, and isn't afraid to use it.

In other words, the exact opposite of who I really am.

"Wondered if you'd be here tonight." The deep velvet voice sends a shiver down my spine.

He's here. Magnolia would never be so bold, but as Seven, I turn away from the bar and let my gaze travel from his boots up his jeans-clad legs to a trim waist, up a black Henley that hugs a thick chest and arms, on up to a jaw covered in dark gray and silver stubble, and finally up to bright blue eyes that crinkle deliciously as he smiles at me. A familiar tug of gossamer string goes taut inside my body.

"Riggs."

He clinks his beer against my whiskey. "Seven."

"You miss me?"

"All week," he answers. "You?"

"Obviously." My belly tightens. I glance away and take another sip, unable to hold his stare. There's only so much of Seven that really works in the face of this man's self-assured presence. I've seen him here almost every week for at least a year, and each time it's the same: a little bit of flirting and nothing more. That's how it has to be; any more than that and I put him in danger.

We turn our attention to Carol, who's kicking the evening into gear with the opening verse of "Shake it Off." I lean against the bar and fight the instinct to curl into myself under Riggs's gaze as I take another sip of the whiskey, letting its burn fortify me. "What are you singing?"

He shifts beside me. "Why? You want to duet?"

I scoff. "You can't handle me."

"That remains to be seen," he murmurs.

Goosebumps skitter across my skin at the thought of giving myself over to him. His broad body hovering over mine, the scrape of his stubble against my neck as he lowers himself down, the way the scruff might feel in other places. I suppress a moan and take another sip, thankful for the dim light. I need to slow down on the drink.

He leans back on his elbows and tips his chin toward the riser. "Africa."

"That's your song?" I raise my eyebrows. It's a lot harder to sing than people realize. Then again, Riggs is a hell of a singer, and I shouldn't be surprised.

He lifts his beer in confirmation before tipping it back,

and I take the two-second opportunity to study him. His closely cropped hair fades into longer strands on top, the perfect length for grabbing onto. The man is the very definition of silver fox, and carries himself in such a commanding way that it's clear he's used to getting what he wants. Outside of this bar—outside of being Seven—I'd never have the courage to speak to him. Even still, I am every bit of the sheltered school teacher when I'm next to him. As though, despite whatever powers I may or may not possess, I'm never on solid ground when he's this close. I'm desperate for the man to shove me against the bar and kiss me senseless, but if he so much as grazed my hip, I'd probably expire from nerves on the spot.

Carol finishes the song and calls Riggs up. He slides his gaze to me and winks. "Wish me luck."

I suppress a smirk. "You need nothing of the sort."

He puts his hands in his pockets as he backs up, the move serving only to highlight the broadness of his chest and arms. The man is a tank.

What I'd give to be run over by him.

"I need whatever you'll give me," he says, then pivots away.

My mouth dries.

He saunters to Carol and takes the mic from her hands with a smile, then turns to address the crowd of about fifty. "I'm going to need some backup from you guys on this one—are you ready?" The crowd cheers, its pleasure increasing as the first memorable notes flow out of the speakers.

I know that Riggs can't see me from his vantage point on the tiny stage, but that knowledge doesn't stop the way my chest constricts when he looks my way and sings. Seven would give that energy right back to him, so I polish off the whiskey and make my way to the front of the crowd just in time for the chorus. And when our eyes lock and the butterflies in my stomach erupt, I let them take flight, reveling in the escape from real life for a little while longer.

RIGGS

RESERVED FOR PRINCIPAL.

The scrawny choir kid who got beat up in high school would be pretty stoked about that sign. He'd be more excited that the Marines blessed him with muscles in his twenties, but being a high school principal would be a close second.

After looking around to make sure no one is watching, I take a selfie with the sign and send it to my pops with a note I'll call him later. He sends ten thumbs-up emojis in response, then a few pink hearts, and a laugh gusts out of me. I taught him about emojis a month ago, and he's excited. That, or one of the residence's nurses has stopped by and is goading him on.

I pocket the phone and jog up the steps to the school. It's a fairly new build, something from the nineties, and I'm told everything inside is top-notch. Sacred River is a small town, though, which means I'm not holding my breath.

Not that I'd have turned the job down. At fifty years old, I was beginning to think I'd never land a principal gig and would forever be the gym teacher and occasional drama teacher, but the opportunity finally came along. It's only two hours from Pops, and only an hour to Al's for my Thursday night karaoke.

Yes. Karaoke. Listen, you can take the kid out of choir, but you can't take choir out of the kid. I love karaoke. Do I have to listen to a lot of bad singing? Of course. But in return, I get to go on stage and sing, and there is nothing better than having a crowd's attention wholly on you when you know you're kicking ass. On top of that, I get to see Seven. And that woman is worth every second of out-of-tune, wrong-word singing I endure on a weekly basis. Not only does she have a killer voice, but she's gorgeous and single. At least, I assume she is. She flirts like she is, and this week, I'm finally going to ask her out. I should have asked way before now, but I've had a lot on my plate with selling Pops's house and convincing him to move into the assisted living community. Naturally, to hear him tell it, it was *him* convincing *me*, but if that's what it takes to keep him happy, then so be it.

I'm about to buzz the doorbell at the entrance to be let in for a quick tour, but Mrs. Hayes is already there to open the door for me.

"Principal Finlay!" she smiles. "Come on in. We'll get you some keys and a swipe card so you don't have to wait going forward."

I give her a broad smile in return. "Thank you, Mrs. Hayes. And please, call me Riggs."

She makes a face. "Absolutely not. I may be old enough to be your mother, but the day I call my principal by his first name is the day I'm on my deathbed."

I hold my hands up. "In that case, Principal Finlay will be just fine."

She sniffs contentedly, settling the matter, then gives me an approving once-over. "Glad to see you're dressed for the job. Good-looking, too. That won't hurt. Follow me and I'll get you settled in."

I smother a laugh and follow her as she toddles to the front office. I'm fairly certain the septuagenarian committed at least two HR violations with that speech, but honestly, I'm glad she approves of the button-down and dress slacks. Pops always taught me to abide by ZZ Top's rule—every girl's crazy about a sharp-dressed man—and it's never steered me wrong. Granted, I've not dressed to chase anyone in a long time, but I pay attention to my clothing. I dress casually only when I'm outside of school, and even then, I take care with what I'm wearing. Thank you, military, for instilling that in me.

We spend the next hour in my new office, then another hour walking the halls while she gives me the background and history of the teachers and students. Which is a nice way of saying she gossips about everyone, seems to know everything, and doesn't hesitate to tell me what she thinks of all of it. By the time we're done, I know that Mr. Dander, the band director, hasn't shaved his mustache since the mid-nineties and it's never been a good look; that Miss Bird the English teacher has been mooning over Mr. Edwin the History teacher for the past two years and she wishes Miss Bird would realize it's never going to happen and move on; and that the new algebra and trig teacher looks too young to be teaching.

Through it all, I nod and hum in all the right places. I make note of the things that actually need my attention, like faculty meeting dates and announcing the new Spanish teacher, and try to forget the things that a principal really doesn't need to know.

"The annual teacher summer party is tonight," Mrs. Hayes reminds me as we round back to the office.

I bite back a groan. I'd forgotten all about it.

"It'll be at my house, as always, and the theme this year is Tiki Teriyaki," she finishes with a flourish. "So you'll need the proper attire. I assume it's in your car?"

"Um," I stall, grimacing at the way her thin eyebrows scrunch and her lips tilt into a dissatisfied frown. How has this old woman already managed to make me feel bad? I thought I was going to be the one in charge, but clearly, that is not what's happening. She's a miniature version of my boot camp drill sergeants. "I didn't. I'll go home and change, and see you there."

She looks at the wall clock. "I suppose that'll be what you have to do," she sighs. "Don't be late."

I'M LATE. Of course I'm late. Because even though I've moved into town, I just got here yesterday and most of my stuff is still in boxes. And despite consulting the spreadsheet that lists the contents of all said boxes, the ones that I needed were not easy to get to.

I look at the flyer on my phone one last time to confirm that it does, indeed, say "beach chic." No idea what that is. Add on that this is the first time I'm meeting the staff, and the pressure is on. I FaceTimed Pops to help me choose my outfit—the man has style, what can I say?—and I'm in simple canvas sneakers, red shorts with blue lobsters on them (because you can never go wrong with conversation shorts), and the show-stopper: a white guayabera button-down. Which, of course, required ironing. Which meant I was looking at my spreadsheet and unpacking a different box. After a moment of deliberation, I throw on a straw fedora and put a pair of Wayfarers in my breast pocket. Here goes nothing.

Twenty minutes later I'm trying not to gape at the massive two-story brick house in front of me as I follow the tiki torch-lined pathway to the backyard. A beautiful kidney-shaped pool dominates the front half of the yard, and lush grass kicks out in the back half. There's a bar to the side decked out with grass streamers, The Beach Boys stream out of the speakers, and dozens of people are milling about. I force my nervousness down and throw my shoulders back. *This is just like stepping onto the karaoke stage. All eyes on you, and you've got this.*

I spot Mrs. Hayes and meander that way, dipping my chin with a smile at anyone who manages to look at me. "Ah, you made it." Mrs. Hayes gestures to the younger woman next to her. "This is Miss Bird."

"English, right?" I extend my hand.

She smiles back politely, and I'm struck by how bird-like her face truly is. "Sarah, and it's American Literature and AP Lit, actually—Mrs. Hayes likes to lump me and Miss Green into the same boat."

"And I'm Miss Green," says the woman beside her. "Ava. English Literature and thank god no AP." She laughs and grips my hand with a firm shake.

Introductions continue for the next half hour, and I thankfully get a beer from Mr. Dander, whose mustache is actually pretty perfect for the man, despite Mrs. Hayes' strong opinion of it. He's on his second or third beer and getting really wound up about the status of the marching band uniforms when Mrs. Hayes interrupts us.

"Someone else got here later than you," Mrs. Hayes *tsks.*

I turn to the person she indicates and nearly drop my beer. Wide, caramel eyes blink back at me in shock. It's *her.*

My throat immediately thickens, but I manage to choke her name out. "Seven?"

Magnolia

THIS CANNOT BE happening. This can *not* be happening.

It's happening.

It *can't*.

Riggs is Mr. Finlay.

My brain whirls as I try to formulate some kind of reaction beyond open-mouthed stupor. The only consolation is that Riggs seems to be having the same response as me. I'm having trouble even contemplating the fact of him being here, and somewhere in the recesses of my mind, there's a squad of mini-mes screaming and flailing at how much hotter he is in the daylight.

Seriously. It's unreal. *He's* unreal, standing in front of me, looking like he stepped out of a fashion shoot despite the shock on his face.

"No, it's not seven just yet," comes Mrs. Hayes' blissfully ignorant response.

He can't let everyone know. It will ruin everything. Panic floods my system and I'm jolted back to reality.

Mrs. Hayes continues. "As I was saying—"

"Of course I'm her!" I hiss. "I'm not a twin. Those are my sisters."

His eyes widen, and it might be because he finally knows something personal about me. "You have twin sisters?"

I wave it off. "Focus. You can't tell anyone that I sing karaoke at Al's. *Ever*."

"But you're incredible—"

"No one. Ever." I growl the last word.

His eyes narrow thoughtfully. "What aren't you telling me?"

A lot. I've built a house of cards on secrets. One wrong move and it will all come crashing down.

"How did I not know you were a teacher?" he continues. "Of chemistry. Ironic, don't you think?"

"Why is that ironic?"

He blinks. "Because we have...chemistry?"

"Not anymore we don't," I shoot back.

I swear his eyes dim with disappointment. After a beat, he dips his chin. "You're right. Probably against school policy anyway."

"No one," I insist again. "You tell no one."

"Mags, there you are!" My best friend Ava appears and hooks her arm through mine. "I see you met our new principal, Mr. Finlay."

Riggs blinks and straightens, transforming from the intense man I'm well acquainted with into a more bland, safe version of himself. Something about the whole thing makes me clammy.

"Miss Green. We have indeed." He smiles, then steps back and claps his hands. "I'll leave you to it—more people to meet." Touching the brim of his hat, he catches my gaze with his own before turning away. The real Riggs is in those eyes, and it's not hard to read the message in them: *we aren't done here.*

I shouldn't feel immediately turned on by the dominance in his expression, or the fact that I'm the only one who saw it. I also shouldn't be ogling his butt as he walks away.

"Miss Rowan, are you making eyes at our new principal?" Ava teases, giggling as she takes a drink of the punch.

"Definitely not." I turn my attention fully to her.

Ava narrows her eyes and inspects my nose, not seeing what she's hoping to find. "He's hot. He's got that whole older-man vibe happening. Too bad I'm not into that kind of thing," she snickers. "You two, on the other hand…"

"Never gonna happen," I declare flatly.

She sucks down the rest of her punch. "Why not? He's single, available, older—what's not to like?"

"How do you know he's single?"

"Mrs. Hayes."

I roll my eyes. I swear, that woman. She is a busybody of the highest order and has been since my own mother was a student. She needs to retire.

Ava looks closer at me. "Are you okay?"

I swallow. I need to remember where I am. *Who* I am. "Let's get more punch."

TWO HOURS LATER, I've managed to avoid Riggs entirely and am cuddled up beside Ava on the back deck's loveseat, giggling drunkenly as we watch sweet Sarah Bird attempt to flirt with Gary Edwin. "It's adorable," I wheeze.

Ava grabs my arm. "Wait. *Wait.* Oh god—she's going for it. Bless Mrs. Hayes' punch!"

I never use my magic, mainly because it never works, but at this point I'm too far gone to care whether anything

Enough. I reach for her and tilt her chin up. The touch sends a jolt of electricity through me, and I narrow my gaze. "That's twice. Talk to me, Seven."

Her eyes, so expressive, flare in the dim light. "There's nothing to discuss."

"Bullshit."

She swallows, clearly nervous, and it releases something in me. Now that I've touched her, I can't stop. My fingers trace her jaw, then her ear. She doesn't stop me. She does the very opposite, in fact, closing her eyes and leaning into me like a cat, practically demanding to be touched.

Don't have to ask me twice. I thread my fingers through her wavy hair and swallow a groan at its silky texture. I tilt my head down, breathing in her clean, floral scent, and my lips are on her hair—literally *on her hair*; when in the world have I ever done that?—before I can stop myself.

She inhales sharply and takes a step back, her expression ruinous. "*No.*" Straightening, she breathes, and repeats herself, more calmly this time. "No. I...can't. *We* can't."

Yeah, well, tell that to the craving that's come roaring out of nowhere, the urgency to pull her to me, the base instinct to protect her and keep her close.

Fuck. I shake my head and clear my throat, trying to come back to myself. She's right. We can't. I *know* we can't. She may be Seven, but she's also one of my teachers. I flex my fingers, then ball them into fists to keep them to myself. "Okay. You're right."

Her shoulders relax.

"But my hand," I push.

Swallowing, she reaches out, and together we watch as her delicate fingertips touch my chest, a gentle spark coursing in its wake as she traces up and down my arm. The woman is electric. Literally. I turn my palm out, everything inside of me crying out for her to thread her fingers into mine, to grant me what I so desperately need. After slowly trailing down my forearm, so slowly I feel every bit of her fingertips as they move, she does.

Thank *fuck*.

I use our clasped hands to close the final inch separating us and lean down again, my lips hovering above hers. It doesn't matter that we shouldn't do this. It doesn't matter that outside this bar, we have entirely different worlds and responsibilities. And it doesn't matter that the light in here is too dim to see the details of her eyes, because I know their whiskey depths are darker than usual, the caramel and oak of them swirling into longing. There's no stopping what I say next. "Kiss me, Seven."

After a beat of hesitation, she tips up, and her lips, soft and sweet, are on mine. A sense of absolute rightness steals over me. There's so much more to this woman, and I need to know her. *Have* to know her. She's behind a shroud of mist, amplifying just how much I don't know. Seven's hand tightens around mine, and I work to deepen the kiss. She doesn't open for me. Instead, she breaks contact and stares at me once more, her eyes searching mine.

Something has shifted. Something intrinsic. I can't explain it, but I know there's something between us. I lean down, needing her lips again, when Carol calls Seven's name through the haze. With one final squeeze of my hand, she withdraws.

As the song begins, it's obvious she picked the song on purpose. "Stand Back" by Stevie Nicks. And sure, the lyrics are pretty straightforward: stand back. The message is clear. The thing is, there's a yearning in this song, too, even a little magic, and as Seven transforms her voice into Stevie's, dropping flawlessly into character, I see the moment she realizes that she forgot about the last part of the song. The part where she has to sing "take me home."

I can't take my eyes off her. I've never been able to, but after that kiss? That touch? Understanding that the woman on stage in black jeans and boots is only one small piece of the person I'm desperate to know?

I'm riveted.

Magnolia

"I NEED TO make it stop."

Clementine startles, a dropper in one hand and a test tube in another. She scowls at me, a rogue dark curl falling out of her bun. "Hello to you, too."

I shut the greenhouse door behind me and make my way to the workbench that doubles as her laboratory. Like me, Clementine takes a more scientific approach to our gifts. "Making more Elysian Blossom essence?" The flower itself is one that only our family can grow, and after first getting the plant to grow any time so she could extract its essence, earlier this year Clementine figured out the original love potion our family was once known for.

She shakes her head. "Working on something else for Mom and Aspen. Why—you got someone you want to use it on?" she jokes.

"The opposite."

She snorts. "Yeah, right."

Okay, I deserved that. Of all my sisters, I'm the one usually fading into the background, never making waves, never causing any kind of real issue. Still: ouch.

Picking up on the pinprick of hurt she delivered, Clementine sets everything down and faces me. "Sorry. Is there a new kid in town who's got the hots for teacher?"

Annoyance flares, and I cross my arms. "Keep it up and none of your teas will be safe."

She snickers. "You're never subtle, and I always know when you've tried. Besides, I'm the one who discovered the antidote to Mom's truth tea, and I'm the youngest!"

I roll my eyes. "Because you were the only one Mom needed to use it on." Untrue. But why let that get in the way of a good story?

"Fine. I need to check on something—walk and talk?"

I follow her outside. We live on five acres of land, and Sacred River runs right through it. Our family was here long before an official town was, and while we *could* fill plenty of gaps in the local history, we've not bothered. Today, most of our land sits on the east side of the river, but we keep a patch on the west to grow very specific plants that need to be over there. Growing up, the scientist in me couldn't stand the reasons that Mom gave to my incessant need to understand. The plants could easily grow on the east, yes, but then they wouldn't work. Work *how?* I'd pressed. To which she'd answer, *"Work."*

Even now, at forty, I still want to know more, but that's not how it goes. The land, the river, the plants, the giant willow tree beneath which so many spells must be intoned… it all just *works*. Best not to look too hard at the Universe. She prefers her mysteries, and no amount of chemistry experiments will get her to reveal what she wants hidden. And I've grown to accept that, to know when I'm beaten.

Doesn't mean I'm going to stop fighting this new issue. Not yet. I need the Universe to drop whatever this is with me and Riggs. That kiss was…well, it was a problem. A big one. The way it felt to have him so close, to stand on the precipice and want so desperately to let myself pitch into the abyss, was terrifying—maybe more than the prospect of hurting the ones I love with my singing. It's been over a week since that kiss happened, and I can't stop thinking about it. I've dreamed about it; only in the dreams I open my mouth and let him all the way in, and his arms wrap around me as he pulls me flush against him. I've stopped the dreams before they go any farther than that, waking up in sweat-soaked sheets and tingling with need.

And those damn sparks. I may be the sister that no one pays much attention to, but I've had a handful of lovers, and never, so help me *never*, have the sparks shown up. I know what those mean, and since I'm not in a mind to maim or kill Riggs Finlay, here we are.

I skipped karaoke last night, and I've been off-kilter all day. I need to sing. I know I do.

Clementine leads me to the river and to the patch of thistle growing there. As she bends to gather it, she wordlessly asks me to grab the mushrooms on the oak tree. I smile, glad I picked up the canvas tote on our way out of the greenhouse, and pick my way through the wildflowers.

Plucking the chanterelles off the tree, I begin. "His name is Riggs Finlay. He's the new principal. There's…history between us. I need him to forget it."

"Forget what, exactly?"

"All of it."

"You know that I'm not the best one to ask, right?"

I look around the tree to where she's crouched. The diamond of her engagement ring glints in the sun, and I take a moment to marvel at how the baby of the family has managed to find love. It's not something that seems to come easily to us. "I know. But you're the one I trust."

"You're not telling me everything." She straightens to her full height, which isn't very high at all, and attempts a glare.

Except for the part where the flowers in the magnolia tree spelled the word *SING*, in capital letters, every time I looked outside, the white of the petals luminescent in the full moon's light.

When Riggs texted me and said he wouldn't be here tonight, I nearly crumpled to the floor in relief. My first thought had been to wonder how he got my number, then I remembered: he's the freaking *principal*, and of course he can find my number very easily. The relief at knowing I could come and sing without having to fight my body's every instinct to wrap itself up in and around him was palpable.

The opening strains of Queen's "Bohemian Rhapsody" come through the speakers, and it feels like stepping under a waterfall. Energy pulses through me, and I swear I can almost see the aura of bright white around me. *This is what you're supposed to do*, the voice whispers to me.

I know. And yet, I can't. Singing around those I love might hurt them, and I'm not willing to take that chance. I've learned my lesson, over and over.

Still, the looks on the faces in the audience are clear. They're happy and light, basking in the glow of my energy. I can actually see it flowing out of me, wrapping around them in stunning hues of bright pink and yellow. When we get to the chorus, I gesture for everyone to sing with me, and the air explodes with purple glitter. It's beautiful, and I drink it in, cooling from the inside out, my chest finally at ease, my body humming happily.

Carol winks at me as I hand the mic back. "Beautiful."

"Thank you—I needed that."

"Clearly. You gonna go again?"

I'm answering before she finishes the question. "If I can, definitely."

"With the way you looked up there and how the crowd responded, of course you can." She opens her arms for a hug, and I step into it, reveling in the feeling of peace and contentment it brings.

Carol has been a constant the entire twenty years I've been here. I'd been driving past the bar on summer break from college, singing in the car because I knew it was safe, and saw the sign advertising karaoke. It became my place on breaks from school, and I've never looked back. I don't know what she does outside of this; I've kept my distance and my heart from her.

I know I should have sung in the car these past weeks. Believe me: I tried. Every time a song came on the car radio, the words wouldn't come. I'd open my mouth, and nothing. My body knows what it needs, and refuses to give it to me.

Grabbing a whiskey from the bartender, I relax into the night. After another hour, Carol calls me back up, and as I approach, she leans into me. "I'm thinking it's time for 'Sweet Caroline'—good?"

I grin. "For you? Anytime."

I step onto the tiny dais and launch into the Neil Diamond classic, hamming it up for the crowd and getting everyone involved with some perfectly timed hand movements. I'm in my element, crooning and swaying, enjoying the give and take with the crowd as we all smile and sing together, and as we hit the final chorus, a familiar face emerges from the crowd.

Ava.

Ava, who is looking at me in utter confusion, and who is also completely riveted.

A delighted smile breaks across her face, and I choke out a cough and nearly drop the microphone. This is bad. *This is so bad.* I manage to recover and keep us going to the end, then sprint out of the spotlight and practically shove the mic into Carol's hand.

"Seven? You all right, hon?" Her voice is low, the huskiness of it warm and concerned.

"I'm…fine," I gasp, then whirl away. I need to leave. Immediately.

"Magnolia!" Ava's voice trails me as I speed away. "Mags?"

I don't stop. I grab my purse off the bar, unable to remember if I paid and not caring, and slam outside.

I'm halfway across the gravel parking lot when Ava's exasperated voice carries over to me. "Magnolia Rowan, I know that's you!"

Nope. No. Not happening.

I speed-walk to my Fiat and wrench the door open, getting in and starting the car. Throwing the car in reverse, I'm about to punch the gas when Ava appears in my rear-view mirror.

"Woman, what the hell is wrong with you?"

I roll the window down and yell. "Go away, Ava!"

She whacks the back of the car. "No!"

"Please! I need you to leave and forget this ever happened."

Whack. "No! There's no reason for this! Why are you running away? It's just karaoke and holy shit, your voice is incredible! Who knew Neil Diamond could sound so good?"

"It's not hard, and *please*, Ava." I poke my head out and around. "Please move."

"Magnolia." Ava is beyond pissed, and her dark brown eyes sear into me as she says, "Put the car in park, get out, and talk to me."

Beaten, I do as she says, frantically trying to come up with a story that's not a lie. I slump against the car, refusing to look at her.

"I have so many questions," Ava says.

I don't speak.

She sighs. "Fine. Did she call you Seven in there? Why are you dressed like this? You never do, and damn, you're hot. Why haven't you talked about singing? Was this the first time you've been here? *Why aren't you looking at me?*" She growls that last part and pokes my chest, her copper skin mottled with anger.

"Ow," I whine.

"Speak."

A giant boulder is on my chest. I can't tell her the truth. I can't. "Take your questions back. And leave. But have someone else drive you. And be careful for, like, the next week."

Her brows slam together. "What in the hell are you talking about, Mags? Or is it Seven?" She crosses her arms.

"Could you please just trust me?" I plead.

She scoffs. "Trust you? No. Not when it seems like you've been hiding something for who knows how long. I thought we were friends. *Best* friends! What is all this?" Her chin wobbles as she waves her hand at me, then she sniffs hard.

My throat tightens. "I…"

A crunch of gravel has us both turning. Standing there is every bit the kind of tall, dark, and handsome man that Ava likes. His gaze is trained on Ava, kind, assessing. "Everything okay here?"

The blood drains from my face. She was here on a date. A date that I didn't know about. How could she not have told me? The hypocrisy slams into me, unrelenting as a tornado. I swallow hard and try to clear the knot of emotion that refuses to budge.

Ava smiles softly at him, then turns her attention back to me. I can read her like a book, and she's heartbroken.

She heard me sing. *What if something happens to her?* "Be careful," I manage to say.

She blinks and thins her lips. "Whatever." Then she turns away.

She threads her arm through the man's, and I know I'll face her soon enough. In the meantime, all I can do is murmur a plea to the Universe to keep her safe.

WHEN I GET HOME, clad once more in a maxi skirt and tee, the kitchen is packed. Mom, Willow, Aspen, and twins Juniper and Jasmine are all there, sitting around the table that isn't big enough to hold all of us but does so anyway. Clementine is noticeably absent; she and Quinton have their own place in a corner of the property. That doesn't automatically mean she's never here, only that we don't see her as much as we used to. It's hard to get my head wrapped around that, despite Quinton having been in our collective lives since February.

Juniper's eyes narrow as they settle on me. "Where've you been?"

The twins are a full decade younger than me, but it's never stopped Juniper from wielding her gift like a champion. Immediately, I envision a filament of shimmering cloth dropping over my mind and gathering my thoughts close, clearing my mind of Ava and singing entirely. I know all my sisters' gifts, and it's second nature to counteract them; keeping my secret from all of them has meant a near-constant use of counteractive activity. I half wonder if that's why my wishes don't work—all my energy is poured into fear.

Mom looks up from pouring a cup of tea. "Sit. Join us."

"What's going on?"

"We're testing a new blend," Aspen says.

I slide into the chair that's appeared and lift a delicate, toile-patterned cup to my nose. Rule number one for living in the Rowan house: never, *ever*, drink the tea without smelling it first. And woe betide the person who can't smell the ingredients that spell trouble.

Inhaling, I catch hints of mint, rosemary, lemon, and dandelion. Perfectly normal ingredients for a tea. *Too* normal, in fact. I sniff again. "What am I missing?"

Jasmine peers closely at me. "You don't smell it?"

I shake my head. "Did you make it?"

Jasmine blushes, the color making her normally hazel eyes turn blue. "I did."

The grin that spreads across my face matches the rest of the family. Jasmine hasn't made a blend in years—not since she accidentally blinded Juniper for twenty-four hours back when they were teenagers. She was so scared that the blindness was permanent that she'd sworn tea-blending off after that. Never mind that it was due to the wish she'd blended into the mix and not the mix itself.

That's rule number two: a Rowan woman's wish is more than a wish. Much, much more.

"So what's the ingredient?" I ask.

"Jasmine."

I arch a brow. Using the ingredient one is named after tends to make whatever is being made much more potent, and that usually applies first and foremost to the scent. I smell it again, and there, just beyond the larger notes, is the sweet fragrance. "Found it!" I say. When I realize everyone is watching me, I set the cup down without taking a sip. "And have all of you tried it?"

All their eyes slide away.

I sigh. "Mom." She's not always the ringleader, but in this case, I bet she is.

When Mom looks back at me, her gaze is unapologetic.

"Clementine is keeping a secret. You're closest to her. We just want to know what it is."

My mouth pops open and then hinges shut again. I was *right*. And so was Clementine, because as sure as she'd have told me, my sisters would have forced it out of me. I fight the frustration down and focus on what's most important: "Jasmine, the first blend you put together in fifteen years and it was a truth tea? Seriously?"

Her blush is deeper now. "To be fair, we all drank it."

"Learned all kinds of...tea," Juniper says, snickering as she takes a sip from her own cup.

Everyone else laughs, but I'm not sold. I push the cup back to the center of the table. "I know she has a secret. She hasn't told me what it is. And for the record, you could have just asked me. We all know that."

Aspen lifts her chin high, defiant and resolutely unapologetic as always. I love her, but one day, my older sister will get what she deserves, and I can't wait for the chaos.

"Aren't you proud of Jasmine?" Juniper asks, clearly trying to keep the peace like always.

I stand, done with the conversation and ready to be alone with my thoughts. "Very proud." I press a kiss to the top of Jasmine's head between the two dark auburn buns she's pulled it into.

"Sure you don't want a nightcap?" Jasmine calls.

I ignore the laughter that follows.

It isn't until I'm in my bed, the room stuffy in the early July heat, that I allow thoughts of Ava to return. And with those thoughts comes a layer of thick, suffocating guilt. Aside from my sisters, she is my oldest and truest friend. Losing her would crush me. For the first time, I think that not telling someone my secret might crush me, too.

What if I told her? The idea is so foreign that I sit up in bed, gasping in the humid air.

Could I do it? Confess my inability to sing around the people I love?

A rush of something awfully close to hope flares inside me, bright and tingling. I grab my phone with shaking hands and blink back the tears that threaten. Even if I'm not ready to spill everything, I need to know she's unharmed from hearing me earlier tonight.

MAGNOLIA

Are you okay?

Her reply is immediate.

AVA

Oh, are we talking now?

MAGNOLIA

Seriously. Are you okay? Like, physically?

AVA

eye roll emoji Of course I am. I'm about to be even better when I let this tall glass of water kiss me. I'll talk to you later.

Also, you are not even remotely off the hook.

I click off my phone, breathing a little easier in the dark.

Riggs

I AM A man driven to distraction.

And frankly, it's starting to piss me off.

I have lived for five decades. I have seen things. Done things. Said and heard things. Lived a whole, fulfilling life. Had my way with plenty of women. *Plenty*. And they liked it.

But none of them—*none* of them—have managed to bring me to my knees with one kiss and a few…sparkles. Or whatever that was. Which is another thing that confuses me and pisses me off.

My hand isn't itching anymore, so…that's good, I guess?

It doesn't matter, though, because here I am, reduced to daydreams and making up reasons to walk past her classroom in the hopes that she might actually be there, despite it being mid-July and no teachers being around. Mrs. Hayes is giving me a shitload of looks and it's obvious she thinks I've lost my mind, and I'm beginning to think she's right.

I leave the school at ten, muttering an excuse about washer and dryer delivery to Mrs. Hayes as I go. The look on her face makes it clear she doesn't believe me.

Probably because it's a lie.

I'm crawling out of my skin with the need to see her. It's Thursday, and I swear if I don't see Seven—Magnolia, whatever, I don't give a shit—at karaoke, then I will flip some damn tables.

So clearly, I need to work this energy off before tonight.

I get in my car and head to the gym to take my frustrations out on the punching bag, when a store I've not paid any attention to catches my eye. *Rowan Apothecary & Books*. That's Magnolia's last name, and Mrs. Hayes has mentioned there are more than a few Rowan women. She also said something about needing to watch myself around them, but given her propensity toward exaggeration, I'm choosing to ignore that.

I like knowing there's a local shop other than a drugstore to get remedies at, so I head inside. The scent of lavender is the first thing to hit my nose, followed by all manner of smells I can't begin to place. There's a palpable sense of calm, and it's bright and warm even though the place is stuffed with dark wooden shelves lined with books and boxes and bottles. Einstein bulbs hang somewhat haphazardly from dark rope along the ceiling, and I gravitate to a table of soaps, picking one up to smell. It's...odd. A dark spice mixed with something salty and briny, and as I inhale again, I'm hit with something approaching serenity, and considering I was ready to explode not five minutes ago, I decide to invest in multiple bars.

A tall, thin woman with long blonde hair appears. Her brown eyes take me in, assessing me with keen intelligence. Something about her is familiar, and I suspect she's one of Seven's sisters. "Can I help you?" she asks.

"Just moved, thought I'd come pay a visit," I reply nonchalantly.

She hums and eyes the five bars of soap in my hands.

"Those are one of our specialties. They give the person using them whatever they need at that moment." She must track my confusion because she continues, "We specialize in natural remedies, and have a wide arrangement of specialty teas for just about everything. You'll also be interested in this table." She gestures to the one beside us. "Stress, sore muscles, that sort of thing."

I narrow my eyes at her. How would she know that's *exactly* what I'm after?

She smiles at my unasked question. "Educated guess. You're the new principal, right?"

Ah. Small towns. I should have known that word would travel fairly quickly. "Yes. Riggs Finlay," I answer.

"Aspen Rowan. I help run this shop with my mother Daphne." She inclines her head toward an old-school soda fountain bar where a tiny woman flits behind it, her pixie-cut gray hair making her appear like a gracefully aged Tinkerbell. "My sister Magnolia is a teacher at your school. Though, you know that."

The heat that warms my chest at the sound of Magnolia's name out of her sister's mouth is concerning. *Be cool.* "Yes, we've met. I'm hoping to see her tonight, in fact."

"Tonight? What's tonight?" Aspen's dark eyes, the shape of them so similar to her sister's that it's unnerving, look at me curiously.

And that's when I remember I'm not supposed to say anything about her singing. Could I be any more of an asshole right now? A nervous laugh escapes me. "School meeting. Wait, is it Tuesday or Wednesday?"

She crosses her arms. "Today is Thursday."

I need to get out of here. Something about this woman makes me want to spill my guts to her, and that is obviously a terrible thing. "That's right. Next week, then. Summer always messes me up." I back away and make a show of holding up the soap. "Actually, I need to go. Great meeting you." I pay and leave before I can make any more of a mess and head to the gym, the memory of Aspen's knowing gaze knotting my stomach.

I GET to the bar a full hour ahead of Carol, and that's saying something. The bartender slides me a glass of water, knowing full well it's too early for me to have a drink, and I tilt it back, downing half of it in one go. Magnolia has ignored every text I've sent since I initially reached out. She gave me one small response of *Thanks* when I told her I wouldn't be here last week, but that's it.

I'm three glasses of water and one trip to the bathroom in when Seven shows up. And dammit, she's even more riveting than the last time I saw her. She's in her usual black jeans and Doc Martens, along with a black, body-skimming tank top that sets off her pale skin in the dim light. Her hair hangs down her back like a silky blonde waterfall, catching the neon blues and pinks of the signs on the walls and shooting them back out.

The fact that I'm getting poetic about her hair is concerning.

The fact that I immediately understood the difference in how she dressed as Magnolia the teacher at Mrs. Hayes' party versus Seven the singer is also a big, fat neon sign of concern. I shouldn't notice. It shouldn't matter.

That fact that she is a teacher and I am the principal: huge problem.

None of that matters as she turns and her eyes meet

mine. Not a damn bit of it. Because my entire body lights up, buzzing in a way I have never felt and I don't like it, but also I crave it, and if this isn't a sign for a fucking drink then I don't know what is. I signal the bartender for my and Seven's drinks, gesturing to her approaching form, and he turns without a word to make them.

"I didn't think you'd be here," she says as she nears.

I force myself not to lick my lips like a wolf staring at his prey. "Think, or hope?"

She considers. "Both."

We take our drinks—she with her usual whiskey neat, and me with a light beer—and sip. As Carol gets the crowd going with Lady Gaga's "Poker Face," I finally speak. "I need you to answer my texts."

"I need you to pretend that kiss didn't happen," she retorts.

I turn to fully face her, and I swear it's like being hit with a magnetic charge. The effort to not touch her is staggering. "Not likely," I bite out. "In fact, ignoring that kiss is so far out of the realm of possibility that it's laughable."

Her eyes flash. "You have to forget it."

I set the beer down. "There's no way I'm forgetting it. And why should I?"

"Because—because…" she sputters. "Just because!"

"I'm going to need way more information than that, Seven." The way her whole body seems to relax at that name coming out of my mouth hits me in the solar plexus.

Up at the front, Carol announces my name. Bonus of being here first, I suppose. Before I can think about it, I bend down and kiss Seven on the cheek, closing my eyes in welcome at the tingle of electricity that comes with it. And there's no stopping my grin as I rise and look at her beautiful, shocked face. "This one's for you," I wink.

I ask Carol to switch the song I initially wrote down, and

while she's irritated at the change—Carol has a pattern and I just messed it up—even *she* can't help but laugh at my choice.

Because I get up there and sing "Never Gonna Give You Up" by Rick Astley. Yep. I straight-up Rickroll Seven and the entirety of Al's right along with her. And not to brag, but one of my many singing talents is the ability to sound a lot like the original singer. So for the next few minutes, I channel a skinny British man with a really deep voice, complete with the requisite air clutches and swoons. Seven doesn't come up from the bar, but if I squint just right, I see the way she fights a smile.

I finish the song to applause, take a bow, and make my way back to Seven. Her eyes twinkle even as she shakes her head.

"You really just did that."

I smile, beyond pleased with myself. "I did."

"You're unbelievable."

"The word you're looking for is 'determined,'" I correct.

She makes a noise in the back of her throat, not saying anything else. For the next half hour, we sit companionably at the bar. When Carol calls Seven up, she doesn't even look at me as she walks to the stage. I don't miss the exchange the women have, and know that Seven's changed her song choice, too.

Is it wrong that I'm excited to hear what she's going to pick?

When the opening bars start, I chuckle as the crowd whoops in delight. This woman is throwing Britney's "Oops!... I Did It Again" at me, and I fucking love it. I don't think twice about nearing the riser and letting her sing right at me, because she swings those hips and goes all innocent lamb while she performs, blinking those whiskey eyes at me as her blonde hair swings.

All of it—*all* of it, the call and response of our song

choices, the fact she didn't hesitate to pick a song she'd normally never sing, the mystery of her insistence on keeping her time here a secret—turns me all the way on. She's irresistible, and I have to have her.

So she can think she's in control all she wants. She's not. It's game on, sweetheart.

Magnolia

"**S**TART TALKING."

My classroom door slams shut, and I whimper at both the loss of air circulation and the unbridled ire of my best friend.

I really, really should have tried harder to explain things to her.

You know, lie.

Make things up.

Do anything, *say* anything, that would have kept me off her naughty list, because when Ava Green puts you on there, it can take years to get off.

Not that I'd actually be able to do it, but still. A girl can dream.

"And don't even think about lying to me," Ava continues. "Your lip twitches, and we both know a mole starts to appear on your nose when you get going."

She's not wrong. That delightful little curse was brought on by Aspen, the eldest sister and inheritor of Mom's goddess-like intolerance of lying.

Personally, I'm a believer in the "white lies never hurt

anyone" camp, but thanks to the mushroom tea that Aspen wished on when we were seven and four respectively, I don't lie. Moles happen. And not the tiny gray rodent kind, either.

I turn around from color-coordinating my class rosters and face the music that is Ava Green. "Hi?" I squeak.

"Hi? *Hi*? Three weeks ago, I saw you pull a damn Celine Dion on 'Sweet Caroline' and all you have to say is *hi*?"

"I texted—"

"No. Shut up." She holds her hand up as her light brown eyes flash, and I realize this must be exactly how she terrifies her students at the beginning of every year.

I close my mouth. I've texted multiple times, and she's deigned to answer, but Ava's clearly been way more upset than I realized.

"We have been best friends for how long?" she asks.

I blink.

"*Answer* me!"

"You said not to—"

"I swear on my big mama's grave, Magnolia—"

"Okay, okay!" I hurry to answer. "Thirty years."

"*Thirty damn years*, Magnolia. We've gone through puberty together. Practiced kissing pillows together. Kissed the Smith twins together. I know your weird witchy-ass family, and I'm still friends with you. So please explain to me how. The fuck. I didn't know that you sang?" Her chest heaves with righteous anger, and I'm momentarily distracted by the writing on her T-shirt: *Surely not everyone was kung-fu fighting.*

I snort a laugh, then swallow it back when she glares. I blow out a breath and gesture to the desks. "Let's sit."

She makes a satisfied noise and angles herself into the seat. "Hate these damn chairs. You better make this good, Magnolia Rowan. I know your sisters."

I've spent the last few weeks trying to decide if I'm really going to tell her, but suddenly the Universe is screaming at me to spill, and you don't live life as a Rowan and not follow the Universe's nudges. Or shoves, as this is beginning to feel like. I've been tempted to ask why the Universe waited until now to allow me to tell the secret, but honestly? I'm scared of what the answer might be.

I take my place across from her and decide to dive right in. *Why beat around the bush* and all that. "I hurt the people I love when I sing."

Instantly, it feels like I'm thirty pounds lighter. The feeling is so real that I have to look down to see if I've changed in some way. No, I'm still here. Still in my Birkenstocks and skirt. Still sporting the silver bangles that never come off.

In front of me, Ava stares. "You—what?" She is the picture of confusion, her brows knitted and eyes traveling up and down my body, cataloging my unpainted toes, standard braided hair, and no makeup. "I don't understand."

I splay my hands. "There's nothing to understand. If I sing around the people I love, they get hurt. I'm not sure they even have to hear me for it to happen." I hold her gaze and tick off the history. "Aspen broke her arm falling out of the *magnolia* tree. Willow lost her hearing for a week. And Clementine—" My voice catches and I take a moment to collect myself. "Clementine's burn is from my singing, too."

Her entire body softens. "Mags, that's not possible. There's no way—"

"Did anything happen to you after you heard me? And don't lie."

"Not a thing."

I stare at her, willing her to tell me the truth. "Honestly?"

She nods. "Honestly. Nothing happened. Not even a hangnail."

I should feel better after hearing that. I don't. "How much did you hear?"

"Almost the whole song," she says, a gentle smile on her face. "You're really good, Mags."

"Yeah, I know."

She chuckles. "Humble, too."

Shrugging, I say, "It doesn't matter. It's not like I'm trying to make a career of it or anything. I just…" I trail off. Then it hits me. "Oh god. Oh no." I surge up and begin to pace.

"What now?" She makes a show of looking around. "Are you going to tell me you ride brooms when no one else is around?"

I purse my lips. "You're funny. Hilarious, even."

"Because we still haven't talked about all of it. Who's Seven, for one thing, and what was with the clothes?"

"So no one knows who I am. We haven't talked about the biggest piece."

"Seriously? There's more? And stop pacing. You're making me dizzy."

"Riggs—"

There's a knock, and the man himself pokes his head in the door.

My breath catches as his bright blue eyes sweep over me, heating almost imperceptibly before he blinks and clears the expression away. "Hi."

Ava's gaze swings to mine, and I can tell she's figured it out. She may not be a Rowan sister, but she's my best friend, and she's no fool.

"Hi," I croak back. *Pull it together.* "Hello. Come on in." I stand awkwardly, completely stupid in front of him as Principal Finlay.

Because whoa. He's in a white button-down with the sleeves rolled up to show off forearms that flex as he opens the door and steps into the room. His chest strains under the shirt, leaving no question as to the defined muscles that lay coiled beneath, and immediately, I picture those strong arms wrapped around me. To make matters worse, he's wearing impeccably tailored linen pants that hug his thighs, and I swear I have never noticed what a man is wearing before Riggs Finlay. Maybe it's because I've been surrounded by men who simply don't care, but Riggs? It's clear he cares. Even the way his thick, dark silver hair has just a hint of product in it to keep the style in place tells me he puts thought into it.

My core aches at the thought of the care he'd put into me. His hands, his mouth, his tongue…

"Hi, Principal Finlay," Ava says from beside me, wrenching me back to reality.

"Riggs, please," he answers, his gaze flicking to her before landing back on me.

"Can I help you?" I want to shove the words back into my mouth the instant they're out. Who says that? Me, apparently.

"I brought lunch." He lifts a plastic bag. "Sorry, Ava, I didn't realize anyone else—"

"Totally fine." She cuts him off, squeezing out of the desk and raising a knowing brow at me. "Call me," she warns with a whisper, "or you're dead to me." She turns back to Riggs. "Good seeing you. I need to get back, though. Those bulletin boards won't decorate themselves!"

She's out the door and shutting it behind her before anything else can be said, and then I'm staring at Riggs, and he's staring at me, and we're in a room, alone. Instantly, the air thickens.

"Seven," he says, his voice low. Sexy.

The way my body lights up at hearing that name from his mouth…holy cow. I pull myself together. "You brought lunch? Let's go eat in the cafeteria."

He growls. Tosses the bag on one of the student desks and closes the distance, a panther homing in on its prey.

I swallow. Brace myself.

Then his hands are cupping my face and tilting it to his. Lips, firm and sure, are on mine a second later, and I hang suspended as that damn spark flares between us. A groan—or is it a whimper?—escapes me as I wrap my arms around him and give in. *Just for a minute*, I promise myself. *What's the worst that can happen?*

I open for him, and he pulls me tight in response, his tongue slipping into my mouth with hot, practiced strokes.

The entire world sighs with me, eager now, because my god, this man can kiss. There's a promise in each slide of his lips, and as his body surrounds mine and pushes me against the desk, I go willingly. My hands explore every inch of his chest, thick and solid and compact, and muscles twitch and flex beneath my touch. Then my butt is on my desk, colored folders flopping to the floor in a messy rainbow, and he's between my legs, his teeth nipping at my lips, his hands stroking down my arms. The air around us buzzes with energy as he cradles the back of my head and increases the pressure of the kiss, absolutely destroying the past year's worth of fantasies I'd built up about him. Heated desire flows through me, centering in my core and crying out for relief.

"Fuck, Seven," he whispers, finally breaking the kiss and leaning his forehead to mine. "I'm sorry. I shouldn't have done that. But fuck me, I just…" he huffs a laugh. "I literally *couldn't* not do it."

"I know," I answer, my voice rough. I can't stop touching him. My hands practically move on their own, feeling the corded muscles of his arms and wrapping around his forearms, the hair on them coarse against my palms. "It's harder here."

"Is that a euphemism?" he chuckles. "Because I am definitely hard."

My gaze drops to his dark pants, and sure enough, they are impressively tented. "No." I can't help the smile that emerges. I tighten my hands against his hips and pencils roll off the desk. "The town. Sacred River."

He nuzzles my cheek, then drops his nose to the sensitive spot right beneath my ear and inhales. The sound that comes out of him as he straightens is half contentment, half frustration. His bright eyes lock onto mine, and I blink away, scooting further onto the desk. He reads me instantly and takes a step back, giving me space.

"The town?" he prompts.

"The magic is stronger here," I explain.

The look on his face is almost comical. "The...magic? Is *that* a euphemism?"

I take a deep breath in, then exhale, bracing my hands on the wood that has seen me through decades of teaching. "How do you not know?"

"Know what?"

"Riggs," I say, exasperated. I should have touched his hair. My hands itch with regret. "If anything, Mrs. Hayes must have said something."

"About what?"

I throw my hands up. "About me! About my family and Sacred River. You've been here for I don't know how long—"

"Little more than a month," he supplies.

"Over a *month*, and you don't know? What the hell is wrong with this town?"

Confusion rolls off him in waves, and his voice is tight as he says, "Will you please stop talking in circles and tell me what the hell is going on?"

"People call us—" I sigh. I almost wish school was already in session. A well-placed teenager would be perfect right about now. "We're witches. Some would say we're not, even one of my sisters swears we aren't, but for all intents and purposes, we are."

He laughs. *Laughs.* As though I have told him the funniest

story ever. I watch him, my lips curled in a smile, absolutely entranced at this man, sunshine incarnate. The restraint it takes not to pull him back to me and kiss him is so freaking intense that it nearly takes my breath away. Then I realize he's slowly closing the distance to do just that, so I force the desire to kiss him out of my head. Sure enough, he stops.

Oh god.

This is bad.

I hiss a silent *Stop it!* to the Universe and focus on the oblivious man in front of me. I need to get control of this situation. Of my intentions. Which have not, for the record, actually *worked*. Not for a very long time. And yet now…

Only months ago, I had a tidy life. Well, lives. Two separate lives that didn't overlap, and it was good. I wasn't totally happy, but I was *fine*. I had my sisters, and I had Ava, and I was fine. Then all this…this *magic* has to start happening.

I don't know which is worse. Either way, it's suddenly here, in my chemistry classroom, that I get to watch both lives smash together like positive and negative particles. Should be explosive.

Sorry. Bad chemistry joke.

I shake my arms out and stand up. Behind me, another pencil rolls onto the floor. "Riggs."

He eases out of the laugh, his eyes twinkling with amusement. "Next, you're going to tell me that Mr. Dander is a werewolf, and I gotta say, the man's canines are a *little* long, so I might believe you."

I bite back a smile. "Mr. Dander is most definitely not a werewolf." *Ask me a specific question*, I urge.

Still grinning, he asks, "Why do you say you and your family are witches?"

Thank you. "Because we can make things happen. Not always directly, but we can…nudge things along. With intentions and spells. Sometimes it's more, um, obvious than other times. But…" I stall, not really knowing how to explain it to someone and not have it sound like I'm a complete lunatic. "Honestly, you didn't hear about us?" I'm still having a hard time believing that literally no one bothered to tell this man he'd moved to the town with the witches.

He tilts his head and studies me, the shallow frown lines bracketing his mouth deepening in thought. "You're serious."

"Yeah," I say softly. "Honestly, I'm surprised. Everyone knows. It's a small town, after all."

"So the apothecary—"

"Yep."

"And the random comment Mrs. Hayes made about magical teas from there—"

"Well," I hedge, "I wouldn't call them magical."

His eyebrow arches. "Then what would you call them?"

I sigh. "Magical," I mutter. "They're magical. Not all of them, though. Not even *most* of them. And it's not like Harry Potter or anything, we're not stocking Eye of Newt and things aren't flying around. No brooms."

He blinks. "You're not joking."

I shake my head. "You need to know. It's…" I pause, trying to figure out how to say this. "Relevant."

"Relevant," he repeats. Motioning between us, he says, "This isn't—Jesus Christ, is this some *spell*?" His eyes go wide as he backs up.

"No!" I nearly bark the word. "No. Not at all." It's worse than a spell. So much worse. How exactly do I explain that?

"I need to sit down." His skin pale, he grabs onto a desk and sinks into it, wincing at the way it pinches his waist.

A pencil rolls his way, and I glare at it. It stops.

I blink, my own breath nearly stopping along with the pencil. *This is new.* I look at Riggs, whose face is buried in his hands.

No harm in trying, right? It's what my sisters have always

spilled on me, and she didn't lead with "Oh, by the way, Miss Rowan, the chemistry teacher, can do more than just chemistry?" I still don't understand anything, and the irony of it all is that no one in town mentions it outright. I went to the drugstore and told the pharmacist I was having some bad allergies, and they suggested I see the women at Rowan's Apothecary for some tea. At the garden center, I said I was looking for some local plants, and the proprietor insisted the Rowan property had the best selection, if I could get them to sell me anything. I went to the library to ask about some books on the history of the town, and instead of mentioning the Rowan witches, the librarian just pointed to the relevant section and went back to helping someone with a job application.

Honestly. It's either that everyone is just so used to it that they don't mention it, or it's not real.

I have a feeling it's the former.

I grimace at Mrs. Hayes. "Happy first day of school."

She waves at me to get up. "Come on! Students to greet, parents to meet."

I haul myself up and follow her to the front, checking my cuffs and straightening my tie as I go. I ease into the hallway, careful not to mess with the flow of students entering from the front. It's a perfectly normal high school in what I thought was a perfectly normal town, but I can't stop squinting at people to see if they're, I don't know, werewolves or some shit.

It's ridiculous.

"Hi, Mr. Finlay!" A student I've never met is waving and smiling at me, her young face almost impossibly fresh and enthusiastic.

Beside me, Mrs. Hayes leans in and says, "That's Claire Jersey. Senior. Captain of the cheerleading team."

I smile at the girl. "Good morning, Miss Jersey."

The girl flushes, ducks her head, and scurries off.

The process repeats for the next ten minutes, Mrs. Hayes feeding me info about students as they pass by and introducing me to others who slow down long enough for her to catch their eye. I've already met the football team, so I get plenty of "what's up, Principal F?" nods as they make their way down the hall.

Eventually, the two-minute warning bell sounds, and the sounds of lockers being shut eases. I put my hands in my pockets and start to walk. A few minutes later, homeroom has begun and Mrs. Hayes is giving the morning announcements, her voice echoing into the empty halls. Already the place smells different, lingering scents of perfume and body spray mingling alongside a distinct 'new school year' smell. New shoes, pencils, backpacks, that sort of thing. It's subtle, but I've taught for so long that there's no mistaking it. Glad to know that even in a town that apparently houses witches, some things never change.

Mrs. Hayes finishes with the announcements, and it's not long before I'm in the science hall, drawn to Magnolia like always. I haven't seen her all week, but it hasn't stopped me from thinking of her, of the way she went soft in my arms, giving in to me as I plundered her lush mouth.

I clear my throat and remind myself I'm the principal. Principals can't have semis as they walk the halls. My dick doesn't get the memo, which is not surprising. When has it ever listened to me when it comes to Magnolia Rowan?

Her voice is clear as a bell, melodic and damn near riding out of her classroom on a wave to me, luring me in. Tingles race over my skin, and I feel like a drunk Disney character, lumbering toward her with my tongue lolling. In reality, I've merely slowed my steps until I'm standing just outside her door, thankful that she hasn't papered over the thin strip of window so that I can watch her.

She's animated, speaking with both authority and excitement, and it's cute as hell. I know, without a doubt, that I'd have a crush on her if I were one of her students. Her hair is up in what I think of as her customary Magnolia braids, only they're a little fancier than usual. French braids, maybe? No makeup. A shirt that says *Why can you never trust an atom? They make up literally everything*, and a long skirt with tiny red flowers on it. Birkenstocks. Briefly, I wonder if her toes are polished, and picture them pressed against my hands as I massage them. I don't have a thing for feet, but I absolutely have a thing for *her*.

"Principal Finlay!" Mr. Dander calls my name from down the hall. "We need to talk about those marching uniforms."

He's loud enough that Magnolia jerks her gaze toward the door, and I give her what I hope is a stern look before turning my attention to the band director. This man may just be my new sworn enemy.

LATER, when I know Magnolia has a free period, I ask Mrs. Hayes to have Miss Rowan come see me. Because I don't know if it's magic or straight-up lust, but if I don't get a taste of this woman, my world will crumble. Not five minutes later, Magnolia appears, a confused look of apprehension on her face.

"Shut the door," I demand.

She does it, a flush rising up her neck as she turns back to me. "Did I do something wrong?"

I couldn't be more grateful for the way this office faces the front of the school and gets the early afternoon sun. It ensures that no one outside can see through the glare, so we're free from any curious eyes.

I nod, my expression deadly serious. Then I say, "No."

She's even more confused, and my dick twitches.

"Come here." I scoot back from the desk. "On this side."

She hesitates.

"Seven," I say, using the name on purpose in the hopes that it lures that side of her to the surface. "Now."

It works, because her expression morphs right before my eyes, going from innocent to siren. Even her posture changes, the self-assurance of her alter ego surfacing in the way she rounds the desk and slides into position before me, her eyes fused to mine.

"Better," I murmur.

"Why have I been called to the principal's office, Riggs?" Her voice is breathy.

I drift my hands to her hips, the cotton of the skirt soft beneath my touch. "Because I wanted to see you," I admit. "And I know it's risky, but I had to." I watch her closely, moving to palm her calves beneath her skirt, still holding her gaze. "Is this okay?"

She swallows and darts a look at the door before blinking slowly.

"Do you feel it?" I ask. "The sparks?"

Her breath hitches as the pulse in her neck speeds up. *That's a yes.* I trace my fingers up her skin, ready to stop the moment she wants me to, swallowing a groan at how silky smooth she is.

"Riggs," she sighs and closes her eyes. "What are you doing?"

"Touching you." I move my hands farther up the skirt, then lean forward in the chair and press my nose to the apex of her thighs, inhaling, so fucking grateful she's let me go this far. She hisses softly. "Smelling you."

"Someone is going to come in." Her voice is strangled.

"They won't. Mrs. Hayes is under strict instructions. Now tell me something," I demand, leaning my head back and moving one hand up her leg while the other traces her skin to the front of her thigh.

Her breathing is ragged. "Wh-what?"

"When you get yourself off, do you use a toy? Or your fingers?"

"Holy shit," she exhales. Her hands clench. "What the hell is going on? We are in *school* ohmygodddd," she trails off.

I let out a low chuckle as I press against her clit on the outside of her cotton panties. Panties that I'm nearly certain are plain and some kind of pastel color. I make a note to buy her some lacy confection for later. Right now, it's all I can do not to yank these down and plunge my tongue into her. "I told you that you could have it your way. I didn't say I wasn't going to have it my way, too, Seven."

"Riggs," she whispers. "Please."

"It's hardly the time to beg, sweetheart. Answer the question." I trace a finger up the seam of her, noting the wetness and aching to taste her arousal. I circle my thumb around the tight bundle of nerves, and her hips angle up as she shifts her legs to open them a little wider.

"Fff-ingers," she whimpers.

"Do you not like toys?"

Her hips swirl, chasing the orgasm I'm absolutely going to give her. She smells so fucking good. "I—*god*, I do, I just…" she squeezes eyes shut and lets her head fall back.

I'm tempted to edge her, and as delicious as that sounds, I can't risk it here. So I press harder on her clit, watching her face to gauge precisely what she likes and following it. "Just what, Seven?" I murmur.

"Mine broke and I can't have it shipped to the house

because my sisters will know," she answers, her voice weak. "God, Riggs, please don't stop," she whispers.

She's right there, so damn close, and even though I know I shouldn't, even though that door could fly open at any fucking second, I do it. I push the cotton aside and plunge two fingers into her, bending them to beckon her orgasm on. She gasps, her mouth popping open with a silent scream as she detonates, her walls clenching around my fingers and her legs shaking with the force of her climax. I think the papers on my desk vibrate as she comes, but I'm not about to take my eyes off her to confirm it.

"There you go," I soothe. "So good, you're so fucking gorgeous." I keep encouraging her, praising her, relishing the way her inner muscles pulse around my fingers.

She comes back to earth and looks at me, her cheeks flushed and rosy, her neck a dark pink. Her eyes are glassy with release, and they heat as she watches me pull my fingers from her and suck them into my mouth.

"Fuck, you taste incredible," I say, my voice husky. "I can't wait to lay you out on this desk and eat you, Seven. Then I'll turn you around and fuck you until neither of us can stand."

She squeaks, and it's fucking adorable.

"Don't have anything to say?" I grin, entirely satisfied with myself, hard as steel dick notwithstanding.

There's a knock at the door, and Magnolia moves faster than I thought possible. She throws on a bright smile and tucks a loose strand of hair behind her ear as she turns to the door, fully in place on the other side of the desk as the door opens and Mrs. Hayes pokes her head in.

"Sorry to interrupt, Principal Finlay, but some parents are here to see you." She doesn't look sorry at all, and it's clear she's not sure what to make of me or Magnolia.

"I was just leaving." Magnolia ducks her head at Mrs.

Hayes. "I'll send you the information for the lab materials." She looks back at me as she speaks, and I swear there might be a glint of mischief in her eyes.

Like I said: fucking adorable.

Magnolia

I BARELY KEEP it together as I pass by Mrs. Hayes, praying to the Universe that the old woman's sense of smell has dulled over the decades. Can't do much about Riggs's office, though, so I send a quick wish for a magnolia-scented breeze to float in and hope for the best.

It's not until I'm back in my classroom and sinking into my chair, my legs still unsteady from the most intense orgasm I've ever had in my life, that it hits me.

I just got finger fucked in the principal's office.

The heat that spreads through my body is enough to incinerate me. I grab my industrial-size water cup, shove the straw in my mouth, and start taking deep pulls of water. I cannot believe that just happened. One minute I'm thinking I'm in trouble somehow—never mind that it's impossible, I make a habit of never doing anything to get in trouble—and the next minute, Riggs is calling me Seven and *smelling* me... and his thumb...and the words out of his mouth...

"I told you that you could have it your way. I didn't say I wasn't going to have it my way, too, Seven."

I cough at the memory, and am whacking my chest and

trying to breathe when one of my star students comes in ahead of the bell.

"You okay, Miss Rowan?" she asks, her brow furrowed as she strides over to me.

I wave her off. "I'm…fine," I wheeze. "Perfectly fine. Thank you."

She hesitates, and as the coughing fit wanes, she seems to relax.

I wipe the tears from my face and take a deep inhale. When I'm certain I can breathe normally, I smile. "How can I help you?"

Suddenly shy, she looks down and mutters her request. "I wanted to ask if you'd be willing to write me a recommendation letter for my college applications."

My heart bursts as I press my hands to my chest. "Sunny, I would be delighted to do that."

She beams. "Thanks. I'm really thinking about botany. Ever since your sister came and presented to the class, I've been looking into it, and it sounds perfect."

Students begin filing into the room, signaling the end of our conversation. "Just get me the info and I'll make sure it's handled. Get it to me soon—no dawdling!" I smile.

She returns the smile and takes her seat, and I force myself to focus on my students for the rest of the day.

AT EXACTLY 3:38, eight whole minutes after school has let out, Ava comes into my classroom. "First day is *over* and it is time for *margaritas* and—" She stops and looks at me, raking her eyes up and down. She points at me. "What happened?"

"Keep your voice down!" I hiss.

Her dark eyes go wide. "What happened?" she repeats, closing the distance between us.

"Margaritas. I'll tell you over margaritas," I promise. Because have mercy, I need them.

It doesn't take long before we've packed up and I'm following her behemoth of a Yukon to our favorite Mexican restaurant. There are two in town, but this one is farthest from the school, which definitely helps make it the favorite. It's also closer to each of our houses, so that's an added bonus.

We clink our glasses to each other and take a sip. I keep going, needing at least half a glass of the sour drink in me before I can say the words out loud.

Ava's eyes get wider and wider as I chug. "Jesus, Magnolia, what is going on?"

Finally, I set my glass down. "Riggs called me into his office today."

She shimmies her shoulders. "Ooh, called into the principal's office," she teases.

I raise my eyebrows.

"Wait. Wait. You got called to the principal's office, or you *got called to the principal's office?*" She looks at me suggestively.

My bracelets clink against each other as I take another massive hit of the margarita. "The latter."

She squeals and bounces up and down in the booth. "Hell yeah girl he is *fine* tell me *everything.*" She angles the straw to her mouth and sips, her entire body wiggling.

"God, I'm so glad you're talking to me again," I sigh. "There's still so much to tell you."

"Yeah, well, it turns out I'm a lot more forgiving with the way my new man is giving me the goods."

I laugh and tell her everything, going all the way back to the beginning of meeting him at karaoke and finishing with today's, erm, *moment*, because the sugar-wrapped tequila has bounded into my veins exactly as I wanted it to, and I am nothing if not an answerer of direct questions.

I am also a lush when it comes to margaritas.

Which maybe I should have thought about before we ordered a pitcher, but too late now.

When I'm finally finished, I'm at the bottom of my second glass and Ava stares at me, trying to make it all make sense. "So you two have flirted for a year, and then you kissed, and then he"—she makes a vaguely inappropriate gesture—"you? In his office?"

"Yes."

"With Mrs. Fucking Hayes on the other side of the door?"

"Yes."

"Ho. Ly. Hell."

I top her glass off and pour more for me. "Pretty much my sentiments exactly."

"Dude is a kinky motherfucker."

I suspect there's way, *way* more where today came from with him, and the text that buzzes through confirms it.

RIGGS

I can still taste you.

"Is that him?" Ava asks.

I smile as a blush stains my cheeks.

She snorts. "Yeah, you keep that shit to yourself. But honey," she reaches her hand to cover mine, "how are you?"

I slam my drink down, sloshing the margarita onto the table. "I'm. *Freaking*. Out," I say, doing some kind of hiss-squeal thing, "and I don't know what to do!"

"Ah, there she is. I was wondering when Magnolia was going to show up."

"It's not just that, Ava! It's…ugh," I moan and bury my face in my hands. "What if I hurt him with the singing?" I peek at her through my fingers.

"Oh," she breathes out, realization dawning. "You like him. *Like* him like him."

I take a slurp. "I don't want to, I swear I don't, but there's this spark thing? When we touch? And it's bad news, because family legend says if there's a spark when a Rowan woman kisses or touches someone, then that's it. Poof. That's your person. So, sure hope you like them."

"Oh god, what if it would have sparked when you kissed one of the *Smith* twins!" Still laughing, she suppresses a shudder.

I make a face at her. "Mean."

She holds her hands up and snorts a laugh. "Sorry, couldn't help myself. Maybe that's not real? Or maybe you two just have a lot of static electricity that has to burn off, and that just happens to be a thing when you kiss."

I stare at her. "You know how ridiculous that sounds?"

She levels her own stare right back. "Probably as ridiculous as a spark indicating your forever love? Even better: it's as ridiculous as the people you love being hurt whenever they hear you sing." She folds her arms and leans back in the booth, entirely too satisfied with herself.

"You're the worst," I groan.

"I love you, too."

We eat, *and* we finish the pitcher. And then there's no way we're driving home, so her new man arrives to pick her up, and Quinton shows up to get me.

He grips my arm to steady me as I fall into the passenger seat. "Damn, Magnolia, you did some damage in there," he chuckles.

I close my eyes and hum. Then I fling them open, because the sensation of being on the ocean is far too intense. "Oh god," I moan.

He laughs again as he pulls onto the road for home.

"You're twisted. I never thought I'd see the day when sweet Magnolia got lit."

"That's the problem, isn't it?" I say. "Sweet little Magnolia. *Never* does anything. *Never* gets suspected of doing the salacious deeds."

"Big word you got there," he grins at me before looking back at the road.

I swat him. "Hush. And it's true. No one ever suspects me of anything. Which is good because whoo, boy, if they knew."

"Knew what?"

I hiccup. "Knew my secret." Belatedly, I realize I've said too much. "Just kidding, Quinton. No secrets. Not here. Nope. I'm sweet Magnolia." Then I sing the words *Sweet Magnolia* to the tune of "Sweet Caroline," followed by a rousing *bah, bah, bah*, and clamp my mouth shut again.

Thankfully, all Quinton does is laugh. "A little Neil Diamond comes out when you're drunk, eh?"

I giggle. "Aw, you're so Canadian."

"Okay, sweet Magnolia," he says indulgently. "We're home. Do you need me to help you inside?"

"Nope." I lurch up and haul myself out of the car. "You're great, Q. Thanks." I shut the door and make my way up the stone walkway to the house. I send a buzzy wish into the Universe for my sisters to ignore me, then head inside and up to my room without anyone talking to me.

It isn't until I'm in my bed, two glasses of water chugged and a good old-fashioned aspirin downed, that I realize I've got a string of texts from Riggs, each one racier than the next. I squint at the screen and force myself to reply.

MAGNOLIA

> I'm very drunk, but all of this sounds delightful.

Three dots, or at least what I think are three dots, appear immediately.

RIGGS

On a school night?

MAGNOLIA

It's all your fault

What you did to me

Who the hell does that

It was so hot though

RIGGS

Oh, my girl is extremely drunk, isn't she?

I think about caring that he's possessively called me his girl, then I swat it away.

MAGNOLIA

Not sure I can sing around you anymore, which makes me sad

RIGGS

Why not?

I wince. "Dammit, Mags," I whisper. "That was stupid." I don't have to tell him the *whole* truth, just a little bit of the truth. He seems like a careful guy. Man. Guy man. Man guy? Whatever.

RIGGS

You still there?

I type the answer before I think too hard about it.

MAGNOLIA

Because I like you too much.

Then I squeal and flop back onto my bed, my heart pounding in my chest. *Crap! I just told him I liked him!*

It feels like I'm twelve all over again, right before I told Andrew Scotts that I thought he was cute. Unfortunately, Andrew Scotts proceeded to make a face and declare that girls were gross, and witches were even more gross, and that since I was both of those things, I was absolutely the grossest.

Obviously, this was before I realized that twelve-year-old boys were assholes. Oblivious little assholes who were mentally still about ten years old and in no way, shape, or form ready for the awesomeness that was girls. Or other boys.

Across the room, something crashes to the floor. I surge upright, heart pounding. Before I can get out of bed, my phone buzzes, so I grab it and squint at the words that swim in front of me.

RIGGS

I like you, too.

I grin at the screen so hard that I probably look terrifying. Then, deciding whatever fell isn't a big deal, I turn my notifications off and fall into a dreamless sleep.

Riggs

I MAY HAVE checked the district's handbook about fraternization a couple of times. And I may have asked Mrs. Hayes to set me a call with the superintendent. And the superintendent, who was apparently a graduate of Sacred River High the same year that Magnolia was, just laughed at my request to "possibly, potentially, date a teacher."

"Mr. Finlay, it's a small town," she'd replied. "It'd be more scandalous if teachers *didn't* date each other."

"But I'm the principal," I said.

"Same difference," she answered. "Go forth and date. Marry. Whatever. We don't care."

So that was settled.

Magnolia's managed, yet again, to avoid any real conversation with me today, but there was no mistaking the flush on her pretty cheeks any time our eyes met across the lunchroom. It was just as adorable as everything else she does.

"What are you doing?"

I jump and nearly drop the yearbook. I swear, the woman

is a ninja. "Mrs. Hayes." I purposely deepen my voice to hide my surprise as I face her. "Just treating myself to a little history lesson."

"In the dark?" She switches on the overhead lights, illuminating the small room off the front office with a fluorescent glow.

"Plenty of outside light." I gesture to the window. It's true...and it's also true that I was planning to look at the years of Magnolia's time here for any clues about her whole *I can't sing around you because I like you* thing.

She gives me a concerned look. "Principal Finlay, is there anything you...need?"

For you not to stalk me? I hold up a stack of yearbooks. "Got everything right here, thanks." I turn my attention back to the thin books in hopes that she gets the hint, and she does. Which is frankly a little miraculous. I'm tempted to turn the lights back off, but figure that would be weird, so I take my treasures back to my office instead.

I know I'm not going to see Magnolia plastered across the pages of the yearbooks, but it's still disappointing when I've flipped through every single year and found her in only six pictures total—and four of those were her class photos. She was, of course, cute as could be, and every bit the little pre-science nerd in training. She even had a version of her braids in one of them. But no hints.

Then I realize that I've not done what any reasonable man with an obsession would do: talk to the best friend. I check my watch and confirm on the schedule that Ava Green is overseeing a study hall this period. "I'm good, Mrs. Hayes," I say as I pass her on the way out of the office. "Just taking a stroll."

I'm fairly certain she huffs.

I barely appear in Ava's classroom door before she's

telling the kids she'll string them up by their toes if they talk and is up and out of her desk to join me in the hall.

"What's up, Riggs?" she asks, giving me a knowing look as she shuts the door behind her.

"That's what I'm here to find out."

Ava crosses her arms. "I knew I liked you," she says. "What do you want to know?"

"Magnolia says she can't sing around me because she likes me too much."

Her eyes widen. "Did she tell you that last night?"

I nod.

She curses. "Margaritas, man. Listen, it's great she told you she liked you—right? Just focus on that."

I narrow my eyes. "You know something."

"I know that it's not my business to tell." Then she looks around and steps closer, lowering her voice. "I also know that I'm not sure I believe it."

My heart plummets. "She *doesn't* like me?" The words are out before I can think about them, and it doesn't take a genius to realize I've revealed my cards.

Chuckling, she says, "No, Riggs. She really likes you."

My shoulders relax. *Thank god.*

"*And* she believes she has good reason not to sing around you. I'm her best friend, and no way am I going to tell you any more than that. The rest is up to you." She cocks her head. "I can hear you!" she yells at the door. When she's satisfied that the class is quiet enough, she turns her attention back to me. "Why are you still here? I'm not telling you anything else."

I hold my hands up. "Fair enough. Thanks for...well, thanks."

She snorts. "You're welcome. Try talking to Magnolia."

I don't bother telling her that I've tried, because she's

already dismissed me and is giving her class hell for talking, leaving me alone in the hall with my thoughts.

A BETTER MAN might tell the woman he likes that he's not going to karaoke tonight. I am not that man. I don't lie or anything, I just...say nothing. *Do* nothing.

I'd be lying if I said it didn't hurt just a smidge that Magnolia didn't so much as glance my way at the end of the school day, when I stood at the door and nodded goodbye as the students and a few teachers, Magnolia included, streamed off campus. But she's Magnolia here, not Seven, and her shyness when she's not in front of the classroom is next-level.

Either way, I'm tucked into my usual chair at the bar with a glass of water when Seven strides in, the very picture of confidence. The transformation is so utterly complete that my brain still has to do some mental aerobics to reconcile that Seven and Magnolia are the same woman.

Seven's hair is out of the braids, hanging thick and wavy down her back. She's in her standard uniform of black Doc Martens, black ripped jeans and a black short-sleeved top. Her silver bracelets—the only thing she seems to share with Magnolia—catch the light as she tucks a strand of hair behind her ear before grabbing the pen from Carol to write her name in the book.

The ease with which she moves, the confidence that practically oozes from her in this setting, is intoxicating. How could I *not* be falling for her?

I know the moment she realizes I'm here. She straightens and stiffens, and I despise myself for a moment. It was selfish to come here. Then she seems to force herself to relax and turn my way. I raise my water glass in an apologetic salute, but then, to my utter delight, a blush rises up her neck and cheeks. I hope she's remembering that the last time we spoke, I'd just made her come. God knows I am.

She saunters toward me, her chin set, her eyes blazing in excitement or anger—I can't tell—and I'm ready for her. I slide off the stool and throw her a lazy grin. "Seven."

"Riggs." Her voice changes when she's Seven, too. Breathier. Sexier. I don't know how I missed it. "I didn't think I'd see you here."

I reach a hand up to cup her face, relishing the tingle of electricity as I stroke her soft skin with my thumb. Her scent is the same, like green apple with a hint of spice. "There's no keeping me away, Seven."

Her eyes bounce between mine, their beautiful caramel depths a window into the war that rages inside her. "I told you that I can't sing around you anymore."

I lean down, the need to kiss her overwhelming every other rational thought. Another spark races across my skin as our lips touch, and somewhere in the back of my mind, I wonder if it has anything to do with her being a witch, but it doesn't matter. Because I'm pulling her to me, breathing her in, sipping up every mewl and sigh she gifts me, and I want so much more. "I'm taking you home tonight," I whisper as our mouths part.

"Riggs, I—"

I cut her off. "There's no stopping this. Whatever it is, I need it. And I think you need it. So we'll sing. And then? I'm taking you to my house and burying my head between your thighs."

She sucks in a breath.

"And when I'm done making you scream that way, I'm going to fuck you till you're hoarse."

Her eyes flash even as crimson stains her cheeks yet again, and it's as though I've captured both women in one. Her chest heaves, and before she can say anything, Carol calls me up to the mic.

I lean down and capture her mouth again, relishing the surprised squeak I earn when I nip her bottom lip between my teeth. "Let's get this night started, shall we?" I wink, gratified at the almost-laugh I get in response.

Carol hands me the mic and inclines her head toward the bar. "You and Seven?"

"Inevitable." I give her a grin and force the word to sound careless, even though whatever it is that I feel for Seven seems as far from that as I can possibly get.

She raises her eyebrows, and I suspect she's disappointed in my answer. I can't worry about that, though, because the opening strains of Def Leppard's "Pour Some Sugar On Me" are starting up, and the crowd whoops in response.

To be clear, I absolutely picked this song on purpose. Like I always have, only now I make them obvious. And before I kick into gear, I make sure to find Seven as she leans against the bar. Because it's her I'm singing to. She's the demolition woman, and I absolutely want to be her man, and I want both of us hot and sticky sweet from our heads to our feet. The song is brutally intense and athletic, especially the way I'm channeling the late eighties arena rock gods and go to my knees for the last round of the chorus, practically screeching into the mic to hit the song just right.

The crowd cheers in response, but it's not their reaction I'm looking for. There, still leaning against the bar cool as a fucking cucumber, is Seven. She raises her glass of whiskey in salute before tossing it back, and doesn't move an inch as she waits for me to return.

"Not bad," she says as I return.

"Not bad?" I scoff. "That was epic, and you know it."

She shrugs, her caramel eyes glittering in the dim light. "Maybe."

I laugh, then pull her to me. She comes willingly, and I dig my fingers into her hips. "You better bring it when you get up there."

She does. She throws another Britney Spears song at me, singing "Toxic" this time, and I can't tell if I should be flattered or worried by those lyrics. She's addicted to me…but who's the one who's toxic? Me? Her? Or maybe I'm overthinking it. Either way, I am all for the way she dances on the small riser, wiggling her hips and sliding her free hand down the side of her body. She absolutely slays the song, and I don't miss the satisfied wink she gives me as she hands the mic back to Carol.

"We're leaving," I state when she returns.

"But—" she starts.

I grab her hand, her skin warm against mine. "We're leaving," I repeat. I leave no room for discussion as our eyes meet.

She jerks her head once in assent, then grabs her things.

Outside, we walk to her car, parked at the edge of the lot near the dumpster. "It's not safe to park here," I say.

She rolls her eyes. "Get off your high horse, Riggs. I have to change clothes when I get here, and that's the best spot to do it. Nothing's ever happened."

"I know you'll do what you want, but for the record, I don't like it."

She huffs a laugh, clearly humoring me, and I drop it.

"Follow me to my house."

She doesn't respond, and I half wonder if she'll actually do it. There's nothing stopping her from driving to her house, and if she does, there's not a damn thing I can do about it.

So I bend to her and capture her lips with mine, crushing

her to me, relishing the shock of the spark as our mouths meet. She tastes of whiskey and a hint of mint. Intoxicating.

I need this woman.

All of her.

"Promise me." I can't hide the urgency in my voice.

I can't be sure, but I think something like resignation flits across her face. "I promise," she whispers.

Magnolia

I F I'M HONEST with myself, it was always heading here. To Riggs's house. To his bed. A full year of stolen glances and flirting, of talking through both the songs we chose and the words we exchanged. Even if he'd never ended up as the high school principal, we'd been on this track for months.

I turn the radio off, needing the silence to steady myself as I grip the wheel and follow him out of the parking lot, my shoulders tense, my legs shaky.

The question isn't whether we'll sleep together. It's whether I can harness my feelings and keep him safe, or whether I'll fail completely and put him in danger.

Thinking of the way his bright turquoise eyes roamed over me in the bar, I have a bad feeling it'll be the former. The sparks, those fucking sparks, have to be wrong. Or maybe they're right and it'll still be okay, because maybe the curse is limited to my family. Which means all I have to do is not marry Riggs and all will be fine.

I scoff. Marriage? *Marriage?* I'm literally following the man to his house for sex, and I've spiraled into thoughts of marriage.

There will be no marriage. Not with him. Not with anyone, if this curse is as bad as I think it is.

I stew the whole way to his house, then shove it all down when I turn into his driveway. He lives much closer to me than I expected him to; his backyard juts up against the edge of our property on the eastern side of the river. The proximity is startling; how did the Universe not tell me about him? How did Clementine not notice him? She walks the property regularly since she tends to it so carefully; there's no missing a man like Riggs in a house right next to us.

And then, all rational thought leaves my head as he unfolds himself from his car and leans against it, waiting for me. The memory of his office slams into me, the way the sun slanted against his back. The way he looked at me as he made me come on his desk, as though he'd do it for the rest of his days. I shiver from head to toe as he waits on me. It's clear what my body wants, what it craves, yet I still hesitate. There's no missing the strength and power coiled in him, the pleasure he could give, but what happens after?

I could leave. The thought is treacherous, yet I turn it over in my mind anyway. I promised him I would come, and I've done that. I *didn't* promise I would stay.

Riggs pushes off his car and strides to me, his thighs flexing beneath dark jeans, his face a quickly fading mask of patience. He opens my door, then leans in and turns off the ignition before I can process what he's done. "Get out, Seven," he commands, his voice low and gravelly.

My own thighs clench together at the roughness of his tone, the way it brooks no argument.

"Unless it's Magnolia," he says, his voice no less intense. "Either way, get out of your car."

I stare at him for a beat and take in the absolute authority in his expression. It's not that he's pissed—not even close. I think he sees right through me, and he knows I want this just as much as he does.

How far am I willing to let this go? Can I give him just my body? Or does giving him my body immediately hand over my heart, too? My…everything?

The seconds it takes me to decide feel like an eternity. I'm on the precipice. I know I am, and I know that whatever I decide is going to change things. Not just for him, but for me. For us. For everyone around me. I don't know how— that's not a gift I have, or even want—but I know, with absolute certainty, that if I get out of this car and go to bed with Riggs, that my life will be irrevocably changed. What I don't know is whether that change will be for better or worse.

"Fuck it." I mutter the words, then launch myself out of the car and into his waiting arms.

I CAN'T TELL you what his house is like. I know the air is cool and it smells like him, woodsy and masculine, and I know it's got hardwood floors because his boots scuff on them as he carries me to his bedroom, my legs wrapped around his waist, his hands digging into my bottom.

"Fuck," he breathes as I yank my mouth away from his and slide my lips to his stubble-covered jaw, nipping a path to his ear and pulling his lobe between my teeth. He shivers in response.

Then we're through a doorway and the scent of him gets stronger. His bedroom. Three more steps and he's still holding me, still letting me have my way with every bit of skin I can kiss. A moment later, he loosens his grip and I let my legs drop, my feet hitting the floor and backs of my legs finding purchase against a bed.

He cups my face and forces me to look at him. The room is lit only by a faintly glowing salt lamp in the corner. "Tell me your name."

I breathe, my eyes bouncing between his. The bright blue is deep now, a navy ocean waiting to take me deep into its inky depths. His touch is feather-light. I know what he's asking, and for a moment, here on the edge, I don't know how to answer.

Yes, you do.

I do. On shaky legs, I give him what's in my heart and prepare to drown. "Magnolia."

He exhales and shuts his eyes, almost as if the answer is too much for him. Too painful. When they open again, they sear into me as he repeats my name. "Magnolia."

And now I'm the one squeezing my eyes shut in pain, because the tender gruff of his voice tells me he's already jumped into the chasm. That he's waiting on me. I force my eyes open and swallow hard, my hands shaking, my heart beating wildly as he kneels before me, untying my Docs and pulling them off. He holds my gaze the entire time, letting me see every emotion that flits across his face: lust, wonder, amusement at the yellow socks with rubber ducks on them that stand in stark contrast to my all-black exterior ensemble.

He skates his fingers up my calves and thighs before undoing my jeans and pulling them down, helping me out of them and discarding them before turning his attention to my black cotton thong.

He growls. "You weren't wearing a thong yesterday."

I shrug, feigning nonchalance. "I have both."

He presses his nose between my thighs, the move so sudden that I grip his shoulders for balance. "You smell so fucking good, Magnolia," he says, then he yanks the panties down and takes me in. His voice is strangled when he says, "Bare?"

My mouth dries. "I…ah, I like the way it feels."

He rubs his nose over me, the move so instinctual that my hips angle toward him. His shoulders rise as he inhales.

"Take your shirt off," I whimper, desperate to have his skin beneath my hands.

He reaches behind his neck and pulls the Henley off in one smooth motion, then returns his attention to my center.

"So fucking pretty," he says, then takes a languid lick up one side of my folds, and the next. "Like velvet. Fuck me." He adjusts himself.

I'm struck mute by the sight of Riggs on his knees, his broad shoulders a golden bronze with a smattering of dark freckles on them. His strength is obvious, the muscles solid. His skin ripples beneath my palms, and the want that rises within me is so intense, so overpowering, that I keen for it. "More," I whisper. "I need more."

Riggs spreads me with his thumbs and licks my clit. My eyes roll back in my head as I grip his shoulders. Flicking his tongue once, twice, and a third time, he abandons all pretense of taking his time. His hot mouth is luxurious, his tongue the bringer of rapture itself, and words fail me again as he sucks my clit into his mouth and pulls me to the edge of reason. Riggs reads me like a book, learning with every lick and stroke the exact type of pressure to apply and where, and it's no time at all before my orgasm is racing to the surface, sharp and sensual, and I gasp his name as I come. His hands are gentle against my legs as they give out, and I fall onto the bed, propping myself up on arms that feel just as limp as the rest of my body.

Yanking my hips to the very edge of the mattress and spreading my legs wide, he drags kisses along one inner thigh as he hums, then the next, before sitting back and taking me in. His hands stroke up and down my legs, his eyes holding mine, unflinching. He pulls all parts of me to the surface, and in his gaze I am whole.

"Clothes. Off," I say, and for as much as I wish they would have come out as a command, they don't. It's a request, a pleading, an absolute need to see every inch of this man's body.

Like a god rising, Riggs pushes up from the floor and quirks his lips. "Wanna see what you're working with, Magnolia?"

My chest heats at the sound of my name—my *real* name—out of his mouth. "Yes," I manage. "Please." I drink him in as he stands before me. Broad shoulders lead to a solid, muscular chest that speaks to decades of living, his skin marked with a smattering of scars and freckles. As he bends to pull his cowboy boots off, his trim waist holding taut as he bends and straightens with the movements, I see the tattoo on his upper left shoulder. "You were a Marine?"

His feet bare, still clad in his black jeans, he comes close to me once again and chuckles. "There is no such thing as a past-tense Marine, sweetheart. Yes, I served, as did my father and grandfather before me. Did wonders for the skinny high school choir boy, let me tell you."

I look up at him and can't help but smile at the idea of this man as a teenager.

"Yeah, see, that look on your face tells me you're thinking I was adorable back then. I was not," he says ruefully. "Far from it."

I sit up and hook my fingers through his belt loops, pulling him close and pressing my lips to his stomach, feeling it flex beneath me. His chest is covered with a light dusting of hair that angles down to a deliciously dark line that I lick as I undo his jeans and push them down. The bulge in his boxer briefs is thick, and before I can pull them down, he steps away, shaking his head.

"Not before I make you come a second time." Eyes darkening once again, he pulls my shirt off and unclasps the plain black bra, then discards it. Running his hand over his face, he whispers, "Fuck, Magnolia."

Goosebumps race across my body, and despite everything, my hands still shake.

"Scoot back onto the bed."

I obey the soft command, the comforter cool against my overheated skin. He follows, crawling to lever his body over mine, then pauses, holding himself in a plank above me and gazing down at me. Pure wonder covers his face. "You are utterly and incomprehensibly stunning."

His words set me on fire. "Riggs," I manage. "Please. I need you."

"Thank fuck." He lowers his body onto mine, and a whimper escapes at the solid weight of him holding me down. I thread my fingers through his silky hair, the strands a dark silver in the dim light of the bedroom, and pull him to me for a kiss. He consumes me, his mouth claiming me relentlessly as his hips rock into mine, the cotton of his briefs providing just enough friction to keep me on edge. Then he moves down, pulling a nipple into his mouth while he palms the other, and I arch into him, hissing softly at the twin sensations of pleasure. He moans in response.

"Harder," I say, dragging my nails over his back. He increases the pressure, pulling my nipple between his teeth and pinching the other, and I jerk. "Yes," I pant. "Like that."

He switches his mouth to the other breast, licking and sucking his way there, then palms my core, the heel of his hand pressed against my clit and his fingers cupping the rest of me. I mewl, and with a low chuckle, he pushes a finger into me. I thrust my hips to meet it, needing so much more than he's giving me.

"Greedy, aren't you?"

"For you," I answer, meeting his navy eyes without hesitation. "Greedy only for you."

"Fuck," he breathes. Then he gives me a second finger, and my eyes flutter back into my head. "Come for me again, gorgeous. I want to see that flush spread all over your body."

This man. He will ruin me, or maybe it's me who will do the ruining, but I can't find it within me to care as he angles his fingers and presses on that perfect spot inside me. I yank his mouth back to mine, needing the connection. Desperate for it. In seconds, a deep sensation of pleasure coils and tightens within me, and my nails dig into his neck, his shoulder. He presses his thumb onto my clit, detonating me, and I explode for him. The pulses wrack through me, my entire body shaking with the orgasm he's wrenched out of me. He works me through it, his lips hovering above my own as I gasp for air.

When I sink into the mattress, boneless, he whispers, "Perfect. You are absolutely perfect, Magnolia."

"You're really good at that," I purr.

His eyes crinkle in a gentle smile. "I'd do it every day if you let me." He sweeps his dark gaze over me, head in his hand. "Every. Fucking. Day."

All I do in response is thread my fingers into the band of his boxer briefs. He helps, and in moments he's naked beside me.

My head empties as I roll him onto his back for inspection. He's achingly flawless. There's no six-pack here, just taut, delicious skin, and a dark trail of hair angling down to a thick cock that makes my mouth water. His legs are relaxed, tensing only when I run my nails over each thigh. I exhale roughly, unable to put into words what I'm thinking, what I'm *feeling*, and he preens under it.

"Not bad for an old man, huh?" he asks, his lips tilted into a half grin.

"You're perfect," I whisper, echoing his words back to him as I catalog the scar on his hip, the freckles on the tops of his legs. I straddle him and bury my nose in his neck, breathing him in as his hands grip my ass and position me right where he wants me. He lifts his hips to slide his cock along my clit, and I moan at the slick, hot intensity of it. I breathe his name, kissing his neck and moving to shift down, wanting my lips on his chest, but he doesn't let me. Instead, he flips us, repositioning himself on top of me as I wrap my legs around him on instinct.

"God, Magnolia," he grits out. "Fuck. Hang on." He stops the rhythmic moving of his hips and leans over to his bedside table, extracting a condom and getting it on in seconds.

I bite my lip as he once again lowers himself to me, then widen my legs as he notches himself at my entrance, both of us watching the movement. He pauses, looking up to me, and there it is. What the spark told me was coming. It's terrifying, and maybe even unbelievable, but all I can think about is the ache of emptiness inside me, the urgency to have him to the hilt, rocking into me. I lift my hips in silent consent, and on a groan, he pushes in.

Bliss.

Pure ecstasy envelops me as he buries himself, sliding in easily as my body welcomes his. I whimper, unable to do anything with the emotions throwing themselves around within me. I tighten my arms around him as his mouth crashes onto mine, and finally, *finally*, he pulls out to the tip and thrusts in again. I moan, deep and guttural, and his hands tighten on me. "Need you," I rasp. "More."

He pulls almost all the way out again, then slams home, and it's everything.

"Riggs," I gasp and wiggle beneath him. "Goddammit. *More*. Please."

He meets my eyes. "Say it again," he growls.

"Say what?" I ask, nearly out of my head. "That I need you? That I don't know what to do with all of this? With you? That you feel so good and if you don't fuck me into oblivion I might unravel on this bed? *Riggs*."

He moves, his hips crashing into mine with the urgency and intensity I absolutely must have. I don't want slow. I don't want sweet. I need this man to fuck me like he owns me, and he knows it, because his hand moves to grip my jaw and hold me in place while he does it.

Over and over he pounds into me, and I welcome it, nearly sobbing with how good, how *right* it feels.

"Tell me," he commands, his fingers curling around my throat.

The sensation is thrilling, and I bare my neck even more. His grip tightens, his hips still pistoning into me. "Riggs. Your cock."

"How good is it?"

"It's perfect."

He squeezes my neck, not enough to cut off my oxygen, but enough to send another wave of goosebumps across me. "More," he urges.

"I need it," I groan, understanding now what he wants. "That thick cock, so good, oh *fuck* Riggs." My voice hitches up an octave as he shifts and hits even deeper inside me. "So deep, oh my god, so fucking good, so good, god, *yes*, please don't stop, please don't stop, please please please." I'm lost to all of it, lost to everything but the feel of him fucking me, wrenching every last bit of pleasure from my body as I chant a string of praise, the words falling into sounds and keening because there, right there, is the abyss, and he yanks me into it without hesitation.

A sheen of sweat covers us as he pulls my leg up and over his shoulder, and somehow, he's even deeper. We shout together, and I come, my body hurling over the edge in a deep, bone-wracking pleasure I have never felt until now. Until *him*. Until us.

Riggs growls again and thrusts hard, stilling and calling my name as his own orgasm falls over him.

I grip him as tight as I can, holding on as waves of ecstasy crash over the both of us, his head buried in my neck, his breath coming in stuttered bursts on my skin.

For a moment, the world stills. And in the recesses of my mind, a voice whispers that I could have this always if I want it. Shivers fly across my body in response.

"Holy shit," he breathes a moment later, lifting himself off me and pulling my leg off his shoulder. "Thank god for flexibility." He looks at me as he says it, and I laugh at the mirth in his eyes.

"Indeed," I answer.

He kisses me then, slow and languid, as though we have all the time in the world. And maybe we do.

It's only after he pulls a fourth orgasm out of me that I realize what a mess the room is in. The salt lamp is on the floor, and the chest of drawers upon which it sat is across the room and nowhere near the bed. The closet door is flung open, and the curtain rod is angled out of its holder on the wall, the curtain itself sliding toward the floor, as boneless as I feel.

Riggs props himself up against the headboard and follows my gaze, then huffs a laugh as he pulls me into him. "Is that your doing, my little witch?"

Warmth floods my chest as I shake my head. "I...have no idea," I say honestly.

He presses a kiss to my forehead. "I beg to differ. Because last time I checked, I'm not able to make things topple when I orgasm."

I don't respond. Later, as I get up and dress, I can't stop the low-level buzz of urgency to be certain he's okay. Can't stop the way my arms tighten around him as I finally leave. Can't stop the worry that tinges my every emotion as I kiss him one last time.

Because of course I've already fallen for him. I was a fool to think I wouldn't. Which means it's only a matter of time before something happens to him.

Riggs

ALL THIS WEEK, I've made a point of standing at the school's front doors at the beginning of the day so that I can meet the students and start learning their names. And I swear that's the main reason I've done it. But I'd be a damn liar if I said I wasn't also trying to get a glimpse of Magnolia each morning as well.

Naturally, she's avoided me every single time.

I'm hoping she's had a change of heart after the four orgasms I gave her last night, though I'm also learning never to assume anything when it comes to Magnolia Rowan. As the kids start trickling in, most of them with at least a nod of hello to me, Mrs. Hayes appears by my side.

"Good morning, Principal Finlay," she intones.

I bite back a smile. She tries so hard to be intimidating around the students, but unfortunately for her, the pastel sweater sets never make for a tough-looking exterior. If anything, the kids simply want to avoid the long conversation they're guaranteed to get into if they so much as slow down in her presence. "Good morning, Mrs. Hayes."

She gives me her usual update: who's sick, who says

they're sick but are probably faking and she can't wait to see the flimsy excuse they bring in, which teacher is late because of a flat tire, and so on. I'm only partially listening as I scan the steadily thickening crowd of people making their way into the building.

Where is she? I can't get last night out of my head. I barely slept after she left—and of course I wanted her to stay, but it was a school night, and I knew I had no chance even as I asked her to consider it.

Her body. Her moans. The way she writhed beneath me. The way she tasted.

"Good morning, Principal Finlay!"

The student's bright voice brings me immediately back to the present, and I dip my chin at the girl and smile a hello. Then Magnolia's car appears at the very edge of the parking lot. She always parks as far away as possible, and now I know why. I wonder how long she's kept her secret from her family.

"What's the story with the Rowans?" I ask Mrs. Hayes, my eyes pinned to Magnolia as she gets out and hefts an oversized tote onto each of her shoulders. It's time I got her to spill.

The old woman slides her eyes to me. "What about them?"

I shrug. "I've heard some rumors."

She sniffs. "Well. I don't like to talk about others, but those women are interesting."

"Interesting?" I prompt.

"I told you about the apothecary, their teas."

"You did," I admit. "There's more to it, right?"

She sighs. "Guess it was only a matter of time. The mom and oldest daughter run it. Really good teas and natural remedies. My arthritis got much better after I started using what Daphne recommended. They're—" she lowers her voice and waits on a break in the students before continuing. "Witches," she finishes.

I've got to admit, hearing the word from Mrs. Hayes makes me shiver in the morning heat. I remind myself that I already knew this. Magnolia made the damn lamp fall off the dresser when she came last night, for crying out loud. I *know* she's special. Then I remember I should act surprised for the old woman. "You're serious?"

Magnolia's nearly at the edge of the parking lot now, having met up with Ava, who is just as laden with bags as she is. It's day three. How do these women have so much *stuff*?

Mrs. Hayes waves a dismissive hand, as if the phrase 'they're witches' wouldn't be world-altering information to someone. "They've always been that way."

Then something occurs to me. We're the Sacred River *Wolves*. "No werewolves?" I feel like an idiot asking, especially since Magnolia already said there weren't. Still, one more confirmation won't hurt.

She laughs. "Principal Finlay. Of course not. Just them."

I grimace. I honestly, truly, with my whole body, hope she's telling the truth. Because it turns out that even though I'm fine with witches, the very idea of a werewolf makes my insides a little watery.

I might need a bathroom.

Magnolia and Ava are at the bottom of the stairs now, and as Magnolia looks up, our gazes meet. I swear a chorus of angels sing. It's the only explanation I have for how the entire world seems to fall away and I forget everything except for the woman looking back at me, her eyes bright beneath dark brows, her smile broad and secretive.

"Good morning, Principal Finlay." Ava's voice lilts in a way that tells me the likelihood of her knowing I slept with her best friend is extremely high.

I clear my throat. "Miss Green. Miss Rowan," I dip my chin at Magnolia.

Her cheeks flush. "Good morning." Her gaze roams my body as though checking for something—what, I can't tell— before she ducks her head and glides past.

I catch her scent, that clean, green apple smell that is distinctly Magnolia, and my dick twitches in response.

The five-minute bell shrieks above us, having precisely no effect on the students or teachers in the vicinity, and I can't help smiling. Because we may have a set of witches in town, but a warning bell is ignored by everyone.

I MAKE sure to swing by Magnolia's classroom before her lunch period, fully intent on eating with her. As the students surge through the door, already over the newness of me and ensconced in the rhythm of high school, Magnolia's eyes lock with mine.

She blooms.

My chest unfurls in response. "Hi."

"Hi," she responds, her cheeks pink and adorable. "Are you…okay?"

"Why wouldn't I be?" I ask. Lowering my voice, I say, "Unless you're wondering if I'm sore from all that sex last night. In which case, I am."

She flushes even more. "Good. Not good that you're sore, good that you're okay. Not that you shouldn't be. I mean, you should be. Okay, that is."

"You're cute when you're flustered," I grin. After making sure no one's in the hall, I reach for the two blonde braids on either side of her head and pull her toward me. A faint spark accompanies the touch of our lips, and I growl as I wrap my hands in her braids. She steps closer to me and loses herself in the kiss, before finally pulling away and fluttering her lashes at me.

"Principal Finlay, is this how you say hello to all the teachers?"

There's my girl. "Keep calling me that and you're in for a punishment."

Her eyes sparkle. "What if I want to be punished?"

I close my eyes and will my dick to stay in check. "Keep *that* up and I'm calling you to the office again."

"Yeah, I'm still not hearing anything that's bad here," she volleys back teasingly.

Well, shit. Now I'm the one who's flustered. I drop her braids and step back, needing a moment to collect myself. She's in another T-shirt and flowy skirt today; the shirt says *If you can't helium, and you can't curium, then you might as well barium.* I raise an eyebrow. "You teaching kids how to get rid of dead bodies in here?"

She snorts. "Wait till you see my Halloween collection."

My heart swells with affection. Why did I wait a year to say anything to her? But we're here now, and that's what counts. "Eat lunch with me?"

The request seems to knock her back. "Wha—eat lunch with you? Like, *here?*"

I grin. "In the cafeteria."

She hesitates.

"I'm not asking you to marry me, Magnolia. Just lunch. At the teachers' table. In the cafeteria."

She clears her throat. "Um. Okay. I, uh, I brought my lunch."

"So we'll stop by the teachers' lounge first." I look at my watch. "Come on. The principal of this school makes the lunch periods *really* short."

She laughs. "Okay."

It's hard not to grab her hand as we walk to the lounge and then the cafeteria. I *am* able to not stare as she leaves my side and makes her way to the table at the front of the cafeteria—so, good for me.

I watch Miss Bird and Mr. Edwin take seats at the table as I grab a tray. Only one seat remains, and I'm gripped by the insecurity of high school all over again. Will she save it for me? How will she do that without everyone knowing she likes me? I mean, she *does* like me, right? Does she care if people know? Do I?

Jesus. I. Am. Fifty. Years. Old.

I am also an absolute wreck over this woman.

Being principal has the distinct advantage of letting me skip through the line, grabbing an apple and something purporting to be lasagna and garlic bread before paying and heading to the table. Where that one seat blessedly remains.

"Is this seat taken?" I ask when I near.

"No," she says, turning from where she was talking to Ava with a soft smile that I can't read. Is she teasing, or shy, or is it something else altogether?

I grin back and take a seat, knowing I've only got about fifteen minutes left.

"Ooh, famous Friday lasagna," she says. "Bold choice."

I pause, the fork halfway to my mouth. "Um. Why?"

Ava leans over. "Mrs. Warner makes it entirely vegan. She's on a mission to prove that kids will eat healthy if it's good."

I keep holding the fork. "And...?" I prompt.

Magnolia grins. "It's good."

I take a bite, far more tentatively than I'd planned to, and it's good. Very good, actually.

Mr. Dander notices me then. "Principal Finlay!" he booms

from the other end of the table. "Ready to see the band at next week's game?"

Coach Ferguson interjects. "Jerry, no one comes to see the band. They come to see the football team."

"I'm looking forward to seeing both," I respond, hoping that settles the matter. It seems to work, and everyone turns back to their lunches. As Magnolia eats her peanut butter and jelly sandwich, I notice she's drinking something other than water. "Is that tea?"

She looks over at me. "It is. Peach mint. Nothing else is in it, though, if that's what you're asking." Her light brown eyes glitter knowingly.

"Why would there be something else in the tea, Miss Rowan?"

Ava leans over. "Seriously? You *never* drink tea from a Rowan sister. Or the mom."

Magnolia glares at her. "I don't do that."

Ava raises an eyebrow.

"I don't!" Magnolia laughs. "Besides, it never works when I do it, anyway."

I polish off the lasagna and take a bite of the bread, which is decidedly less tasty. "Good to know."

She lowers her voice for the next part, making me lean toward her. When she speaks, her breath hits my neck. "I really don't mess with teas. Well," she hedges, "rarely. Mostly never. My sisters, on the other hand..." She straightens and smiles.

I'm trying hard not to be, well, hard. Because she's teasing me, and it's downright adorable. "Go out with me tonight."

I swear the entire table quiets, but my attention is only on Magnolia, who I'm fairly certain notices, too, judging by the way she squirms in her seat and reaches for her drink.

Ava loudly asks, "Coach, how's the team looking this year?"

A faint blush covers Magnolia's cheeks as she presses her lips together and looks around the table, where they've all turned to hear Coach Ferguson rhapsodize about the football team's offensive line. Swinging her gaze back to me, she nods. "Okay."

"Okay?"

Her leg presses against mine beneath the table. "Okay."

Magnolia

CLEMENTINE SITS CROSS-legged on my bed, methodically shooting down every single outfit I pull out of my closet. "Mags, come on. Surely you've got one thing in there that's not screamingly school-marmish."

I side-eye her. "Screamingly schoolmarmish? From the woman who habitually wears aprons and lab coats over T-shirts and shorts?"

"I said what I said," she sniffs. As she pulls her thick dark hair back up into a bun and secures it with a pencil, she peers around me. "Wait a minute."

Instantly, I'm on alert. "What?" I survey the room, half expecting a bird or some other woodland creature in here. It's happened before. She's like a warped Disney character some-times, I swear it.

Clementine gets off the bed and pushes me aside, reaching into the depths of my closet to pull out a black dress I bought online one night when I'd had too much of Willow's Take A Chance tea. "What is this delightful little number?"

Honestly, I'm just glad I keep all of Seven's clothes in a

completely different drawer that no one thinks to look in. "Willow's fault," is all I say to Clem.

She holds the dress up and looks at me. "Remember when you had me speak to your classroom on super-short notice *and* I was hopped up on love potion?" she says, a familiar spark in her eyes.

"One, that was a favor, and two, you were not hopped up on love potion."

She laughs. "I was *definitely* hopped up on love potion. That and the memory of Quinton's mouth between my legs."

"Clementine!" I squeak.

"What?" she asks, eyes innocent and wide. "It's true."

My cheeks are on fire. I don't need those visuals. "You agreed to talk to my class before Quinton even got here."

"Well, when I *did* speak, I was not in my normal state of mind."

"Irrelevant to the conversation at hand."

"I did you a favor, and you will now return it." She holds the dress up. "Put it on."

"No." I barely resist stomping my feet.

She sighs. Loudly. "Please?"

I try the last arrow in my quiver. "Even if it works, I don't have shoes to go with it."

"Mags. You live in a house with five other women. We'll find shoes. Now, please try it on?" she wheedles, clasping her hands beneath her chin and making the worst attempt at begging I've ever seen.

I know when I'm beaten. I take the dress and change into it, and even as I'm pulling it on, I know Clementine's going to make me wear it. The scoop neck screams for someone to look at my breasts, and the soft, stretchy material hugs every part of my body, showing off curves I never let the world see. I mean, sure, Riggs has seen me naked, but I feel much more exposed in this dress.

"Oh, you're *definitely* wearing that," Clementine announces.

Fifteen minutes later, I'm surrounded by a miniature glam squad—or torture army, depending on your perspective. Juniper sits on the floor, painting my toenails. Clementine does my makeup while Willow curls my hair. Jasmine scrolls her phone and stalks the chef of the restaurant we're going to, mumbling incoherently while occasionally looking up and barking instructions to one sister or another.

I'm exhausted. And right as I'm about to beg all of them to please stop, Juniper narrows her eyes at Clementine.

"Spill it," Juniper commands.

Clementine keeps her attention on the eye shadow palette, not answering, even though we all know she's the one Juniper is talking to.

Willow pulls a strand of my hair into the curling iron and expertly coils it around. The woman is a genius with hair and always has been. She cuts all our hair, for goodness' sake, but has never once considered becoming a stylist. "We all know you're keeping something from us." Her voice is light and airy like always.

"And considering how much you hate secrets…" I prompt, falling right into the pattern.

"It's not time yet," Clementine says, bending around and applying mascara to my eyelashes. "I promised, uh, someone, and I can't break that promise."

The rest of us hum as one, generally communicating that we consent to her not talking about it yet, but also that she's got a short window of time before we all come at her with everything we've got.

Which, when you're talking about a family of witches, is considerable.

"I know, I know," Clementine says, a tiny smile kicking up on her face.

Finally, everyone is finished. My toes are dry, and I'm in very uncomfortable high-heeled sandals courtesy of Hazel's closet, who hasn't lived here in years but is the most footwear-obsessed of all of us. My blonde hair, which is usually in braids or hanging in limp crinkles, cascades in gorgeous, full waves halfway down my back, and my makeup looks amazing. My eyes have never looked this good. The dress is simple, yet effective. After a thorough inspection in Jasmine's full-length mirror, I declare, "I'm a knockout."

"Heck yeah, you are," Clementine says.

"This guy won't know what hit him," Jasmine agrees. "Even though he picked the wrong restaurant to go to."

"Let it go, Jaz," I warn.

She holds her hands up innocently. "I'm just saying."

The doorbell rings, and Clementine holds her hand out to stop me. "I'm getting the door. After what y'all put Quinton through, this man needs at least a fighting chance."

"I had nothing to do with that," I point out.

"It was just *tea*, Clementine!" Willow retorts as the rest of us snicker.

I take a few deep breaths and smooth my hands over my dress. I shouldn't be nervous. It's Riggs.

Precisely. It's Riggs.

Whose voice is so amazing it does things—deep, body and soul things—to me that no one else can.

Who flirted with me as Seven for a year.

Who is my boss.

Who finger fucked me in his office two days ago.

Who gave me the best orgasms of my life last night.

Who I more than like, and thus, who terrifies me.

My heartbeat kicks like a mule inside my chest as head downstairs, the rest of my sisters in hot pursuit. The sound of Clementine saying hello and welcoming him in drifts up, and the only thing on my mind is to keep him from accepting a cup of tea. When I appear at the top of the stairs and his eyes land on me, the look that crosses his face when I come into view is one that I am dead certain I'll never get over.

Because his eyes flare, then darken as he takes me in. His gaze caresses me as I continue down the stairs, starting at my cherry-red toes, wrapping around my bare calves and up to my thighs, hugged tightly by the black dress in all the right places. He lingers around my hips, then moves up to my breasts, chest, neck. When his bright eyes finally meet mine, I exhale.

Wordlessly, he moves toward me, holding his hand out to guide me the rest of the way down the steps. A small spark tingles as we touch, and his lips quirk into a knowing grin. When I'm on the ground, three inches taller thanks to these ridiculous shoes, he cups my face and pulls me to him for a kiss. I'm dimly aware of all my sisters around us, but the feel of Riggs's lips and the tenderness of his hands wipe every trace of embarrassment I might have had away.

His eyes are pools of deep navy as he leans his forehead onto mine and whispers, "You look incredible."

I smile. "Thank you."

He smiles broadly in response and steps back, then seems to see the rest of my sisters. "Hello," he chuckles.

I make the introductions, and then, because of course one of them just has to, Jasmine offers, "Would you like some tea?"

"He would not," I answer, shooting daggers at her.

Riggs glances at me. "I don't?"

My sisters snicker. "You know you don't."

"Maybe I do," he teases, grinning at all of them.

"Maybe he does," Jasmine agrees, then holds her hand out to him.

Right as I reach out to stop him from taking her hand—

which he was absolutely about to do, *dammit,* Jasmine!—the door opens and Quinton walks in, breaking the spell.

Quinton's gaze immediately finds his wife's. "Figured I'd find you here." Then he turns to Riggs. "Quinton Henry."

"Riggs Finlay," comes the response, and they shake hands.

"Don't drink the tea," Quinton says.

I laugh. "See? He knows."

Quinton's expression is rueful. "Yeah, I drank the tea. It all worked out, but seriously, be careful in this house. Also, Magnolia, you look amazing."

"Doesn't she?" Clementine swoons.

"It's just peppermint tea, you know," Jasmine says.

I snort. "It's never *just* peppermint tea with you. Riggs, we should go."

He crooks his arm for me to thread mine through. "Then let's go."

I glance around at my sisters, and each of them grins back at me. Clementine whispers into my head, *"He's hot! Have fun!"*

It's not until we're in the car that I finally get a good look at Riggs. And yes, he's hot. He wears dark slacks and a pale purple button-down, the color making his tan skin and eyes pop, his sleeves rolled up like always. His dark gray and silver hair is perfectly mussed, and the crinkles around his eyes when he looks over and smiles are panty-melting.

"Hey, gorgeous," he murmurs, then leans over the console for another kiss.

I don't hesitate, meeting him and inhaling his scent. I'm hit with a wave of pure lust, and a primal groan makes its way out of me. "Are you sure we need to go to dinner?" I whine.

His answering growl makes me clench my thighs. "I like you like this. And yes to dinner. If only because you're going to need your strength for what I have planned for you tonight."

THE FOOD IS DELICIOUS, but not nearly as delicious as the man sitting across from me. For the first time, I learn about the man behind the karaoke singer and high school principal. I learn about his pops and the apparent horde of octogenarians knocking down his door at the senior living facility on a near-daily basis. I learn more about his years as a skinny kid in high school choir and his service in the Marines. How his mother, a first-generation college graduate who emigrated from Greece, was the guiding force in his life until she passed away too early. How karaoke started as a way to kill the boredom in the barracks, then a way to get dates, and then a way to sustain his sanity as he made his way through those first few years of teaching, and then his solace when his mother passed.

I tell him about growing up with six sisters and our mom. The way Ava and I became best friends in elementary school and were inseparable after that, despite the built-in friends that my sisters were for me. I tell him about the pranks we played on each other growing up, and how they've only gotten more sophisticated now that most of us are in our thirties and forties.

"Pranks with tea?" he asks teasingly.

"Way more than that. In a way, the pranks were practice—learning what our gifts were in a safe space." They learned, anyway. I learned I essentially had none.

He tilts the rest of his wine back, his Adam's apple bobbing as he swallows. It's even more erotic watching him in this small booth than it was at Al's. "Are there more of you?"

I tilt my head. "Witches? Sure. Our particular family is spread across the country, and we come together once a year for a Gathering."

He shifts in his seat, patient and curious.

In the not-too-distant past, I would never have shared more than this with someone outside my family. But he deserves to know what he's getting into. What could happen. I've spent most of my life scared of hurting the ones I love with my voice, and it needs to stop. "There's a lot to explain."

"Of course there is," he teases. "I'm the guy who moved here thinking witches weren't a thing. And yet, here you are."

"You need to be prepared," I warn.

"For what?" He leans forward.

I wave a hand at myself, then him. "Me. Us. If there *is* an us—which," I swallow, nerves taking hold, "Which I'd like if there was. So, I need to explain things."

He gets the server's attention. After we order espressos and a slice of chocolate cake to share, Riggs looks back at me. "Okay. Explain."

My palms are sweaty. That reminds me. "Remember when you asked why your hands had been itching after we touched?"

His full lips quirk up. "How could I forget? It felt like a bad recreation of that old wives' tale about getting money, except it was constant, and I most definitely did not get rich."

My cheeks heat. "Our family was spelled many, many years ago that, when we touch someone who's interested in us, regardless of whether we're interested in them, their palms itch any time they think of us."

He coughs. "Of course. Did I say constant? I meant inter-mittent."

"Sure you did," I grin. "Lucky for you, and the many before you, we've been able to make the spell less, um, intense. We can't totally make it disappear, though."

"What about Quinton?"

"Hmm?"

"He and Clementine are married, right? Did he have that whole hand-itching thing?" he asks, taking a bite of chocolate cake.

"No, but he and Clementine were affected by our family's love potion."

His eyes go wide. "Love potion? You're not serious."

I nod solemnly. "I am. And before you ask, no, you've never been exposed to the potion, or to anything else by me or my family."

His shoulders relax as he says, "That's good."

"I'm not doing this right." I hold my palm out. *Take my hand,* I urge.

He reaches out, almost without noticing, and a tiny bit of guilt niggles at the base of my skull for kickstarting his initiative.

"The reason no one can know about my singing is because," I swallow and gather my resolve, "I was cursed."

RIGGS

"CURSED?" I PROBABLY say it too loudly, but I can't find it in myself to care. Even though I mainly want to panic, I'm oddly...peaceful. Then I look down at our hands. "Are you—are you doing something to me right now?"

Her cheeks pinken. "Not really, but sort of?"

I pull my hand away, and instantly, my heart rate increases. I grab her again, and instantly there's a nudge of calm. "That's a hell of a trick."

"Honestly, it never works," she muses, her eyes on our threaded fingers. When she lifts her gaze, her whiskey eyes are utterly guileless. "You're changing me, Riggs."

I think of the way she inadvertently destroyed my room last night. "Is that a good thing?"

Her hand tightens on mine as she swallows, and her voice is husky as she answers, "I don't know."

I signal the server to pay, and as we head out, I rest my hand at the small of her back. The spark does its thing, of course, and I go with it.

I hold the car door open for her, then pull her to me

before she can slide past. When she looks up, I ask, "Can I take you home?"

She hesitates. "You need to know everything, Riggs."

She's right. I know she's right. Even still, I lean my nose to the curve of her neck, needing a hit of her scent like an addict. "Then tell me there," I murmur, already knowing that nothing she says is going to change my feelings.

Am I confused as hell? Yes. Does it matter? I don't think so.

"Magnolia." I speak softly against her ear. "I'll be good. I promise." She shivers against me, gooseflesh rising on her arm. "I promise," I repeat.

"Okay," she relents. "But we're talking before anything else."

I keep my hand on her thigh as I drive. It's silky-soft, yielding to my touch, and every cell in my body tells me that *this* is right. *This* is what I'm supposed to do. I have to assume there's nothing magical about it, even though the way her touch calmed me earlier...but no. I was on this path way before now. At the house, I take her hand and lead her inside and to the kitchen. "Drink?"

"Water. I'd like to function in the morning, and it turns out, wine and forty makes that a lot harder to do," she says ruefully.

I chuckle and hand her the glass. "Wait till you hit fifty," I wink, then gesture to the living room.

She leads the way and I enjoy the view, watching her hips sway as she moves through the dimly lit house like she belongs here. It's easy to see, too: we'd come home from school and make dinner together, talk about our days, the kids who were driving us bananas and the ones we were so proud of we could burst. I'd massage her feet while she graded chemistry assignments, and eventually, we'd tumble into bed at some early hour so that we could explore each other's bodies for ridiculously wonderful lengths of time.

I'm still lost in the fog of possibilities when we sit on the couch and she takes off her shoes with a wince. It's instinct to pull her feet into my lap and begin to massage one of them. The moan she lets out, her head falling back to reveal a freckle right where her jaw meets neck, makes my dick twitch.

"That is the most exquisite feeling in the world right now," she whimpers as I press a thumb into the arch of her foot. "Oh my god."

I grin at her sounds of pleasure, absurdly happy that I can do this for her. That even in the face of her about to tell me things that might completely change everything, we can still do something so normal. "Your feet are tiny." Another moan escapes as I push her toes back, stretching the foot, then take each toe and rub and pull it.

"Holy shit," she mumbles.

Now I laugh. "Weren't you going to tell me all your secrets, Magnolia?"

She heaves a contented sigh, her head still back with her eyes closed. "Say that again, only this time make it a command."

"What?" I ask, confused. "Why?"

"Because I can't lie," she answers, then moans again as I take her foot in both hands and stretch it down, pointing her toes like a ballerina's. "I mean, I *can* lie, but Aspen made a wish once that I'd grow moles if I did. My *god*, your hands are magic."

My eyebrows hit the ceiling. "Moles? Like, freckle kind of moles?"

"Yep."

"Your sister cursed you to get *moles* if you lied? Damn.

That's harsh," I chuckle. "I grew up an only child, so this is wild."

"Just do it," she urges, meeting my gaze. Then she holds up a finger in warning. "If you stop rubbing my feet, I'll riot."

So I do it. Searching her beautiful, nearly hypnotic eyes, I say, "Magnolia, tell me all your secrets."

She blinks slowly and takes a deep breath. "Thank you."

"You're welcome, I think," I laugh softly, then take her other foot in my hand.

"The reason I can't sing around anyone is because I've been cursed."

I go still. There's that word again. *Cursed.* "Explain." I start back on her foot at the look she gives me.

"I remember a lot from my earliest years," she continues. "Most people don't remember anything before they're five or so, but I can recall memories as far back as age two. They're fuzzy, and just outside my reach in terms of true clarity, but the thing I remember most about those early years is how I'd sing with the birds. They'd circle around me as I toddled around outside, and we'd sing together. I couldn't *talk* to them or anything, but I could definitely sing with them. I'm not sure if that was my gift, exactly, but I was always at my purest, like I was my whole self, when I sang. And it was like that for many years."

I press my thumb into the arch of her foot, watching her eyelids flutter in pleasure. "So what changed?"

She shrugs. "That's what I don't know. There was a Gathering when I was sixteen, and things started happening to my family if I sang around them after that. Little things at first— they'd drop something, or trip, or some other kind of...mild chaos. Then, it got much, much worse. Aspen fell out of a tree and broke her arm, Willow got an earache so bad she lost hearing for a week, Mom sliced her hand open. The worst one was Clementine. She burned her arm when an experiment she was conducting exploded."

I've slowed down on her foot, but kick back into gear when she finally looks back at me. I don't know what to say, don't know if there's anything *to* say without sounding like a condescending asshole. But she needs me to speak, for some kind of comfort to come out of my mouth. "I..." I flail. "Jesus, Magnolia. I've got nothing. How—" I pause, wondering if I should say it, then dive in anyway. "How can I help?"

At that, her eyes fill with tears.

"Oh, no," I panic. "I didn't mean to upset you. Please—"

"It's not that," she cuts me off. "It's—no one's ever asked me that. Like, ever." She chokes out a sob.

My heart twists painfully. It's clear she's barely holding herself together, and I can't take it one more second. I pull her over and into my lap, curling my arms around her and squeezing. How, in a house full of women, has she not found comfort? *Because she's not told them.* God. I tighten my hold on her, covering as much of her body with my own as I possibly can. "I'm here, Magnolia. Whatever you need, I've got you."

At that, she loses it, a keening wail erupting from her as she grips my shirt in her hands. I don't know how much time passes as the grief wracks her, and it doesn't matter. I hold on tight, pressing my lips to the top of her hair and rocking her as she sobs and cries. I marvel at the reversal, how I've gone from worried and tense in the restaurant and needing Magnolia's physical touch to stay calm, to being the one offering comfort.

"It's okay," I murmur against her temple. "We'll figure this out. I don't know how, but we'll figure it out."

She begins to quiet, and as she takes a shuddering exhale, I thread my fingers through her silky hair. Finally, she whispers. "Thank you."

"Hey." I use my finger to tilt her chin up and meet her eyes. This close, they're flecked with gold, bright with tears and devastatingly beautiful. I am so gone for this woman that it's not even funny. "Never apologize for that. Letting your emotions show, being brave enough to be vulnerable with me, is a gift that I will never take for granted, Magnolia."

Her chin wobbles and she sniffs again. "You—you mean that?" Her voice is small, unsure.

I touch my lips to hers, keeping them there as I cradle her head. "One thousand percent, my little witch."

She squeezes her eyes shut and a lone tear escapes. I kiss it away, and when another appears, I kiss that, too.

"What can I do?" I ask. "Tell me what you need right now. We'll start there."

She looks back at me. "Take me to bed."

"You're in luck. I'm an expert cuddler."

"No," she says, her hand pressing against my chest. "I don't want to cuddle, Riggs."

I pull her hands into mine and raise them to my lips, kissing each of her fingertips. "I'll give you whatever you want, Magnolia. And I want you to know how honored I am that you've trusted me with your truths. Your tears. I don't take any of it for granted. Not any of it."

Holding my gaze, she wraps her fingers around mine, then slides my palms over her breasts and down her waist. "You're a wonder, Riggs Finlay."

"I don't know about that."

Wordlessly, she leads the way to the bedroom.

We start slow, peeling off each other's clothes before standing naked, pressed together, as our hands wander. The only light is from the salt lamp, back in its rightful spot and bathing the room in a gentle peach glow, as I sink to my knees in front of her.

"Riggs." She breathes my name out, then runs her fingers through my hair.

At first, all I can do is bow my head, overcome with emotions I'm not ready to name, wanting nothing more than to protect her, keep her safe, and bring her every pleasure. I run my hands up the backs of her knees and thighs before grabbing onto her ass and pulling her to me and looking up. "Tell me what you need."

"You."

I shake my head. "No, Magnolia. You already have me. Now tell me what you *need*."

She hesitates, so I lean my mouth close to her pussy and breathe gently on it. I don't touch. "Make me come," she whispers. "With your mouth. Make me come."

"With pleasure." I press my nose to her and inhale. She smells so fucking good. And when I taste her, spreading her apart for my tongue, she's so damn sweet. I lick and suck, taking my time to tease her, to learn what she likes and what she loves.

"Bed," she gasps, taking the two steps back and onto the bed.

I stand and watch, taking in her body as she situates herself on the mattress and looks back at me. I pump my cock once, needing the relief, and her eyes darken as she watches. "You like that?"

She wets her lips. "You are incredibly sexy."

"No, Magnolia—that's *you*." I crawl onto the bed and kneel once more before her. "Spread for me."

Her eyes sparkle, all sadness gone for now, and I feel like a goddamn hero. I've not even gotten started.

I descend, taking her pussy into my mouth like a starved man, and dive in. I use only my tongue, reaching up to gather her breasts in each of my hands and squeezing. Her pelvis lifts, and I go with it, sucking on her clit as I pinch her nipples. She jerks and gasps, and I take her to the brink. Bringing my hands back to cradle her thighs, I lick and suck until she's writhing beneath me, her legs clenched around my ears.

"Riggs," she whines. "Please."

That's my cue to stop. I ease up, letting her feel the heat of my breath for a moment, then taking a lazy lick of her.

"What—*fuck*, what are you doing?"

I can't help the grin. I know she's fully lost control when she starts cussing. "You asked me to make you come."

"Right," she breathes, her chest heaving. "So do it. Make me come."

I take another lick up her center, swirling my tongue once, twice around her clit. Feeling her tense. Then I stop. "I will. When it suits me."

The whine that escapes her is almost enough to make *me* come. And even though I'd give anything to sink into her, feel her warm and wet and beautifully tight around me, it's not time.

Magnolia brings a hand to my hair and threads her fingers in, then yanks. "Make. Me. Come."

I shake my head. "Not yet." I travel kisses from her hip to her soft belly, up to her breast. We moan together as I pull a nipple into my mouth, and she wraps her arms and legs around me.

"Fuck, Riggs," she groans, her voice deep and sexy. "That feels so good."

I swivel my lips, my cock sliding against her wetness as my eyes roll back in my head. She bucks beneath me, chasing her pleasure, and I let her get close again. Right when her rhythm starts to unravel, I lift my hips and pop off her breast.

Her eyes open and find mine. "*Riggs.*"

"Never been edged before, have you, sweetheart?" I smirk.

She's breathing quickly and her nails dig into my back. "Please," she exhales roughly. "*Please*."

I slide back down her body, worshiping her pale skin, finding and kissing every freckle on her stomach, then her thighs, before finally bending her knees and spreading them as far as they can go.

I look up at her. "Tell me something, Magnolia."

Her eyes meet mine.

"How many times have you come in one night?"

"Fuck," she breathes out, her body flushed, her hair tangled on the pillow beneath her head. She's beautiful. Devastating.

I run a finger down her thigh, then skate it over where she's desperate to be touched before running it up the other thigh. "Answer me. How many times?"

"Last—" she swallows. "Last night."

I lift an eyebrow. "Four?"

She jerks her head in a nod as her hips swirl, seeking friction.

"How many times do you want to come tonight?" I ask.

"As many times as you'll let me."

A slow smile spreads across my face. "Oh, now *that* was the perfect answer." I lean down and lick her, delighting in the sharp intake of her breath. The sweet taste of her pussy. Her arousal. "And since it was so perfect," I lick her again, swirling my tongue around her clit a little harder than before, "I'm going to let you have your first orgasm."

With that, I increase the pressure, bearing down precisely where I've learned she needs it. In seconds, her body tenses, her legs fighting to clamp together from where I've got them spread.

Above me, she groans. Her hands grasp for purchase, one finding my hair and another digging into the mattress. I loosen my grip on her legs, and she bucks and writhes, her hips undulating as I suck. Finally, on a guttural moan, she comes, her thighs clenched around my head, her hand pulling at my hair. As she comes down, I ease up, and finally, she relaxes, her legs and arms going limp.

I wipe my mouth on the sheets and kiss my way up her body, noting the flush that's spread across her breasts, her chest, and her neck. "You," I kiss her shoulder and lick up to just beneath her ear, "are exquisite."

She brings my mouth to hers, demanding and gentle at once. I settle between her legs, and again she wraps herself around me in what's quickly becoming my favorite position. We're pretzeled together, a tangle of limbs and tongues, and as she scrapes her nails down the back of my head and neck, I shudder with pleasure.

"God, Riggs, I—" she stops, unsure.

"Talk to me," I urge.

After a moment, she says, "I need you. Need *this*." Keeping her golden-flecked eyes on mine, she reaches between us to wrap her hand around my cock. "Inside me. *Please*."

I shift so I can grab a condom, fully intent on giving Magnolia whatever she wants, but she tightens around me.

"No. I don't want anything between us. I need all of you," she says.

"Are you sure? I've never—"

"Me neither. I'm sure." She widens her legs and guides me to her entrance.

And that's it. I'm done for. When I slide into her, the bliss that surrounds me is out of this world. "Fuck, sweetheart," I moan, letting my forehead rest against her collarbone. "Oh my god."

It takes everything in me not to say the words that demand to be let out.

Magnolia

S OMETHING HAS BEEN building inside me from the moment we first met, slowly but surely, from the very beginning. Every look, stolen or otherwise, every word spoken and sung, every touch, all leading here. I should have seen it.

I don't know what it is. Not yet. But it's there. Growing inside me, *changing* me. Maybe it's whatever gift I've had buried inside me. Maybe it's something completely different. Whatever it is, it's here.

He pushes into me, taking my breath away, and something shifts. I tighten my grip on him, digging my nails into his skin and hooking my ankles behind his back. Goosebumps erupt across my body as my neck arches into his waiting teeth, and when they sink into the tender skin beneath my ear, I barely recognize the guttural moan that escapes me. "More," I bite out. "Please, god, Riggs—*more*."

"Magnolia," is his only response, his voice dark and utterly ravenous.

The salt lamp falls with a crash onto the floor.

Then he moves. He thrusts into me, deep and glorious,

locking in, filling me beyond anything I have ever felt. Maybe it's because I've never had more than a passing care for the men and women I've slept with, but this. *This*. There's a lightness to the way it feels, a *rightness*.

The feelings he's pulling out of me as he sinks into me, over and over, his breath hot, his tongue slick against mine. The way he shifts us, cradling my entire body as he moves us onto our sides, then he's pushing into me from behind, his hand reaching around to circle my clit. The position unlocks a new level of euphoria, and the sweet heat of another orgasm begins to swirl.

"Come for me, Magnolia," he urges. "Let me feel you fall apart."

I move my hand to join his, both of us touching me, circling my clit, as he strokes into me deep and hard. His breath comes in pants, and I turn my head to take his mouth with mine. A spike of bliss shoots through me, then another, and another, until I'm groaning into his mouth as I come.

"There we go. Fuck, the way you're gripping me. Pulsing around me. You are everything, Magnolia. *Every*thing."

He's nowhere near done. As my orgasm wanes, he shifts us again, going onto his back and pulling me on top of him. His eyes are navy in the dim light, his gaze rapturous, and something else that both terrifies and calms me to consider. His hands skim my waist before digging into my hips. He licks his lips. "Ride me, sweetheart. Take me exactly how you want me."

I do. As I stare into his bottomless eyes, I go somewhere else, and I take him with me. Because even as we move with each other on his bed, in his room, we're not there. Not really. We're above and around and beneath and within, our hands entwined, my hair falling around his head, his own neck arching as I lick and bite his skin, taste the salty sweat of him, smell the woodsy scent of him, and my god, my *god*.

He pulls a nipple into his mouth, sucking hard, and I hiss with pleasure. I'm seconds from another orgasm. "Riggs," I breathe.

He rolls us, his eyes flashing as he growls, "Not yet."

I whimper. "I...can't...stop it," I gasp with every thrust.

Our breaths are fast and hot, utterly and completely feral, and he reaches behind my head to grab a handful of hair at the base of my neck. "Not *yet*, goddammit Magnolia, *fuck*."

"So good," I groan the word, my voice pitched low. The pain of it is exquisite and perfect, and my walls begin to tighten. Panting hard, our skin coming together over and over, I dig my nails down his back as Riggs pounds into me and finally loses his rhythm.

"Now," he grits. "Come *now*."

We shout as one, the words unintelligible as the orgasm pours over us, shuddering against each other as we hold on, his face buried in my neck and my arms and legs locked tight around him. For a moment, there is nothing but this, the coming together of our bodies, the bliss of sensual pleasure, the feel of Riggs spilling inside of me.

Finally, the orgasms subside, and we loosen our grip on each other. Riggs presses the softest of kisses on my neck, then chin, then forehead, then nose, before pulling back to look into my eyes.

"Magnolia."

It's all he needs to say. Our lips meet on a sigh. This time, the kiss is gentle, and the promise it holds is so deep that it almost takes my breath away.

As I breathe out, the closet door swings open.

THE SUN IS HIGHER in the sky than it usually is when I wake up. Beside me, Riggs is propped on pillows against the headboard as he reads a paperback, and it honestly takes me a minute to get my act together because this man is fulfilling a fantasy I didn't know I had.

First of all, he let me sleep.

Also, he's wearing glasses.

Reading.

While naked.

Ask me how I know.

The pristine white sheets are draped deliciously low on his hips, giving me a view of that beautiful divot that I have never before seen in real life. Right above that, he has a freckle and a scar that I'm betting is from chicken pox, and god, how is he so beautiful it literally makes my chest ache? I mean, I can understand the throbbing need between my legs, no matter that the man ravaged me last night, but my chest, too?

Speaking of chests. I sweep my gaze over his. All I want to do is lick him from hip to nip.

I snort a laugh, thoroughly amused with myself, and Riggs smiles down at me.

"Someone's in a good mood this morning," he says affectionately.

I sit up, letting the covers fall, and his eyes darken. "Just thinking about how I want to lick you," I admit.

He tosses the book with a flick of his wrist and has his glasses on the bedside table in under a second. Then he yanks me on top of him, my legs straddling his hips seamlessly. I squeal and prop my hands on his chest to steady myself.

"You may begin," he intones.

"Begin what?"

He fights a smile. "The licking. Anytime you want. I'm all yours."

I laugh again, but it stops as quick as it came as his hand snakes between my legs.

"Fuck," he whispers. "Magnolia. You're soaked."

I wiggle against him, suddenly overcome with need. "Now, Riggs."

Wordlessly, he lifts me up and onto him in one smooth movement, and my eyes roll back in my head as he fills me. "My god," he rasps.

I moan in response, unable to form words. He's deeper this morning than he was at any point last night.

His hands latch onto my hips, and he begins to move us. I'm on top, but he controls everything, lifting me up, back and forward as he thrusts up and in. I thread my arms over his shoulders and meet his mouth for a kiss. It's perfect. All of it is perfect.

When we come, we come together.

Later, after a shower where he washes me head to toe, he makes us breakfast tacos with fluffy eggs and slices of avocado topped with fresh pico de gallo, all in warmed street-style tortillas.

And I know, without question, that I'm in love with this man.

The tacos help, obviously. But really, I love him. And it's terrifying, because I'm certain it puts him in danger.

His eyes, back to their aqua brightness in the light of day, sparkle at me from across the kitchen island we're eating at. "What?"

I finish my last bite and prop my chin in my hands. "You."

He looks around, then points a finger at his chest. "Me?"

"Yeah. You."

He smiles and lays his palm up for me to take it. I do, and the spark—that damn knowing spark—tingles through our hands. He looks down meaningfully, then back up to me. "You ever gonna tell me what that means?"

There's a part of me that wants to skirt the question. A different part isn't afraid at all anymore, and that's the part I lean into. "That we're...meant to be."

His face goes slack for a second, and a wave of regret washes over me. Have I said too much? Gone too far? Then he smiles, big and broad and so bright I nearly squint in the face of it. "Really?"

A giggle bubbles out of me. "Really."

He squeezes my hand, then releases it to sit back in his chair. His mouth opens, then closes, then opens again. And closes.

"Rendered you mute, huh?" I tease.

"I...yeah," he huffs a laugh. "I guess you have. Give me a minute. This is good—I promise you I'm excited—I'm more than that. I just...shit. Really?"

"Riggs," I chide. "That was a fantasy book you were reading earlier. I know you can figure this out."

His eyes widen. "Wait. Are we, like, *mates*? Holy shit, are we *mated*?"

I hold my hands up and laugh. "Easy there, buddy. We're not mates. That's fiction. But we're...something. I don't have a word for it. My sister or mom might, but yeah," I say softly. "Something."

"Is it bad that I want to call my pops and tell him I have a mate, just to fuck with him?" he asks, mischief dancing in his eyes.

I nearly spit out the water I've taken a sip of. "Riggs!"

"That's a no, got it," he smiles.

I shake my head. "Who are you, and what did you do with the slightly growly man I know?"

"That guy didn't have a *mate*, Magnolia!"

"Oh my god. I've created a monster."

He slides off his stool and walks around the island. I turn to him, and he steps between my legs. It's harder than it should be to ignore the way my body reacts to him, and the playful energy flowing off him isn't helping. "This isn't all magic, Magnolia," he rasps, his voice low.

It isn't a question, exactly, but I shake my head anyway. "No. It's the Universe acknowledging what's already there. Or what *will* be there. There's no magic here."

"Except for my cock, right?" He wiggles his eyebrows. "*That's* magical."

I bark out a laugh and kiss him. "Hate to say it, but I don't think your dick is receiving any sort of magical talents."

"All natural, then. Good to know." He chuckles and kisses me again. "My amazing, beautiful, talented beyond belief, witchy, nerdy—ow," he says as I swat at him, "chemistry teacher Magnolia." He exhales roughly, then pins me with a stare. "I love you."

I hitch a breath.

He cups my face, and a thumb strokes my lower lip. "I know it's probably too soon to say it, but I think I've loved you from the minute I laid eyes on you. Certainly from the minute I heard you sing. You enrapture me. Magic or no magic. Sparks or no sparks. I will do whatever it takes, will be whoever you need, as long as you let me love you."

My heart has wound around itself with every word out of his mouth, growing tighter and tighter, and now, it simply bursts. I pull his mouth to mine, pouring every emotion into the kiss I can possibly pour, hoping against hope he can feel what his words mean to me. How can I tell him how much it means to me that he's said all of this?

How can I tell him that he may have just signed my death sentence? Or his own?

I say it anyway. Because I have to be brave. I'm scared of what's coming next, yes, but not scared enough to keep these words to myself. He has to know. I break the kiss. "I love you, too."

My scalp tingles as Riggs pulls me tighter to him, my legs wrapping around his waist as he lifts me and carries me back to the bedroom to ravish me once again.

It's not until much later, when I'm putting myself together in the bathroom before going home, that I see what's happened.

Slowly, so slowly that I can't tell how long it takes, I raise my hand to touch the silver streak that now runs through my white-blonde hair.

Magnolia

I MANAGE TO avoid every sister as I bolt upstairs to my room to grab the journal I'd long since stopped writing in. It's buried in the back of a drawer stuffed full of skirts, the leather binding smelling just as delicious as always. A gift to each of us from Mom, the black ink on the creamy, thick pages is visible only to me. It can hold as many pages as we need it to, and only ever appears to be a slim, tidy journal to anyone other than the owner. Mine is a beautiful, glossy green, bringing the leaves of my namesake tree to mind. Which was, of course, purposeful.

My entries begin at age five, when clearly I thought I was at the height of my witchy power. Tales of singing with birds, watching tadpoles in the river, and fights with my sisters abound. As I get older, the entries get more mature, focused on the usual things a normal girl would be focused on—fitting in and boys—but also worries that only a witch would have. Things like the truth spell my sister put on me and the many concoctions I drank to counteract that spell (all failed), or the tea pranks we played on each other that turned hair purple or made armpit hair grow as long and thick as a boa constrictor overnight.

My entries were long and frequent, but once all the harm came to my sisters, the entries came to an abrupt halt. I'd wanted to be done. Done with all of it: being a witch, being susceptible to curses, the near-painful need to sing that had to get out or make me sick…all of it.

Now, as I stride to the willow tree near the edge of our property, I'm thinking of one particular entry that I need to look at: the last one.

The one I'd asked the Universe to wipe from my memory as soon as I wrote it down. And once I'd written it, I shoved it in the drawer and tried to forget about it. Until recently, that's been enough.

But now?

Making sure no one is around, I lean against the willow and slide down to sit beneath it. It's quiet under here, cooler. There's no real grass to speak of, but the dirt and moss are soft. The magic is gentle here, and as I blink, wisps of vibrant lime green flow between the branches, following the leaves as they sway in the breeze that never seems to stop around the tree. Never in my forty years have I seen it.

I rub my eyes, wondering if it's a trick of the light. It's not. The wisps are still here, ebbing and flowing, deep and verdant, then bright and vibrant. As I watch, they float to me, swirling and dancing through the shade until they meet my fingers, then wrapping up and around my hands and arms before disappearing into my skin.

I close my eyes and choke back a sob, unable to do anything but *feel* in this moment. I've missed this, the simplicity of the magic. The beauty of it, the pure generosity of it.

It's only now that I even remember that I missed it, and at that realization, the tears flow freely down my cheeks, hitting the green of the leather in my lap and darkening it, sinking into the journal like their own entries.

It takes a while before I'm able to open the journal. I start a few entries back.

SEPTEMBER 10

Something is wrong and I think it's Kera's fault. The ceremony for our Sixteenth Gathering was two nights ago, and it should have been the best night of my life. But she brought a boy, and when he wouldn't stop looking at me like the slimy perv he clearly was, she freaked out. Cornered me, accused me of trying to steal her boyfriend, and swore she'd get back at me. Wouldn't listen when I told her I didn't want anything to do with the guy.

The next night, when we were all around the bonfire for the final evening of Gathering celebrations, all she did was stare at me, her lips moving silently as she gripped something in her hand. I felt a prick of something against my neck, but ignored it.

Now it's been a week, and every time I sing, things happen. Not in a good way, either.

SEPTEMBER 15

It's bad. I have to sing or I feel bad. But I think it might be hurting my sisters.

OCTOBER 1

Aspen heard me. She broke her arm.

OCTOBER 30

I'm done. I can't do this anymore. Mom's been hurt. Willow's been hurt. They've all gotten hurt in one way or another. And Clementine...my god. I'm done. No more singing.

I'VE BARELY MOVED READING these. I don't remember any of this—not really. Not the thing about Kera.

All of this...this *pain* because of jealousy? Ridiculous, petty jealousy over a stupid boy? My stomach churns, and the taste of iron fills my mouth. It's disgusting.

And it explains so much. The way she always stares at me, even now. What must she see when she looks at me? Someone she broke, probably.

A kernel of something hot and angry takes root in my chest, and somewhere far in the recesses of my mind, a small voice says I shouldn't worry. That I should move on, and forget, and forgive.

Yeah—no. I welcome the anger. Let it sit and whirl within me, seep into my pores like the magic itself.

With the wisps of magic still dancing in the shadows around me, I take a deep breath and ready myself for the final entry.

NOVEMBER 15

This is the last time I'll write in here. Whatever has happened to me, it's mine and mine alone to deal with. Maybe it was Kera, maybe it wasn't, I just don't know anymore. It doesn't matter. All I know is that I have to sing, but every time my family hears me, they get hurt, and their injuries got worse every time they heard me.

And I know that I can't ask my sisters to help me fix it. Clearly—whatever this is, it is aimed at me and me alone. This is my problem to solve.

So with these final words, I call on the Universe to make my family forget I ever sang. I call on the Universe to protect them from me, to separate my sisters and mother from me as much as possible in both thought and action. And I ask the Universe to wipe this from my memory, because it hurts. All of this just...hurts.

I'm done.

ANGER, red-hot and fiery, blooms within me as I let the journal fall from my grip and wrap my arms around my knees, burying my head in the cocoon it makes.

I want to give in. To swim in the darkness of fury and blame, to point a righteous finger at Kera and push every piece of sadness and disappointment and worry of the past decades at her. And god, it is so tempting. I play it all out in my head, the way I'd tell my sisters, the way we'd plot an epic revenge plan to go down at the Gathering that's coming up.

I won't. I'm better than that.

Well, I'm a *little* better than that. I know enough that if— no, *when*—I take her down, it'll be with my family by my side.

I wipe the tears away and read the last entry again. In a way, I've done this all to myself. The distance from my sisters and mom...all me. All by my own doing.

The kernel of anger flares again within me, but I tamp it down. Getting angry won't do any good. I need to think.

This is why my sisters never asked me for help. Never sought me out for anything, magical or otherwise. This is why Aspen and Mom never...god. This explains so much. I was an idiot to ask the Universe for such a thing. And that the Universe granted it tells me just how upset I really was when I asked. It's unheard of for a witch to voluntarily sepa-rate herself from her sisters. I mean, sure, I've lived with them these past nearly twenty-five years since the curse, but that's it.

Last night, getting ready for my date with Riggs, had been the first time anything like that has happened with me and my sisters. Even at Clementine's wedding, I'd felt removed from everyone, as though I was on one shore and they were on another. Not that they knew that. The dual memories cause tears of pain and gratitude to prick at my eyes, and I let them fall. Because it's time I felt *everything*. And it's past time I stopped separating myself and started figuring out how to fix this.

With my sisters.

Magnolia

THE FIRST PERSON I want to see is Clementine. I have a feeling about something, but I need to actually see her to know if it's true. I step out of the willow tree's canopy and am at her cottage in minutes, banging on the door as if my very life depended on it.

And, in a way, it kind of does.

"Hang *on*, for crying out loud!" she says, then opens the door. Her eyes are wild, her face is flushed, her shirt's on backward, and I'm positive that those pants aren't hers.

"Your hair!" she exclaims.

I wave it away. "Doesn't matter. What matters is you're pregnant."

"Wha—" she starts, then gapes at me while I smirk, wholly satisfied with myself.

"Clem, what's...oh," Quinton comes up behind her, shirtless and in some very, *very* tight pants.

I point at them. "Q, are you wearing Clementine's pants?"

He looks down, then back up. "Uh...Clem, you wanna take this?"

Finally seeming to come back to herself, Clementine

yanks me inside and shuts the door, then whirls on me. "Forget your hair. Who told you? How do you know?"

I laugh. "So it's true? Oh, Clementine," the tears threatening to come yet again, "I'm so excited for you two!"

She lets me wrap her in a hug, then mutters, "Yeah, well, you also just barged in on sexy time with my husband, so this better be good."

I release her and take a closer look. "Ah. Explains the pants," I motion between the two of them. "Sorry about that. Nice legs, Q."

Clementine swats me. "Eyes off my hot chocolate, woman."

Quinton snorts, "Nice one, babe," then ambles off.

Clementine watches him leave, clearly watching his butt. When he turns out of sight, she finally looks back at me. "How did you know?"

I take a breath. "It's a long story, For now, I'll just say that I'm getting my magic back."

Her mossy eyes widen as she grabs my arms. "What? Getting it *back*? That means you lost it? When? Where? How?"

I laugh and loosen myself from her overly strong grip. "I needed to see you to know if I was right."

She raises her eyebrows. "You're right, but you're still missing something."

I raise my eyebrows even higher. "You mean the fact that you're having twins?"

She shrieks and punches me.

"Ow!" I yelp, cradling my upper arm. "Why are we resorting to violence?"

"Because you're ruining my fun!" She gears up to punch me again.

"Whoa there, little sis." I open the front door with one hand and hold the other up to shield myself while I scoot out. "I'm not going to tell anyone—I promise," I say.

"You will if they ask," she pouts.

I consider that. "Nope," I say. "I won't."

Quinton reappears with a peanut butter and jelly sandwich and hands it to Clementine with a flourish. "For my love," he says, winking at her. As she takes it and shoves what I swear is half the sandwich into her mouth like an unhinged monster, Quinton turns to me.

"We planned on telling the family at a Sunday dinner soon. Can you keep it under wraps until then?"

I nod, grimacing as my sweet baby sister shoves the last quarter of the sandwich into her maw. "Good lord."

Quinton chuckles. "Yeah. She's kind of...voracious."

"Bedroom. Now," Clementine demands behind him.

I watch her pivot and head toward their bedroom, yanking off her shirt as she goes. "Is she at least going to brush her teeth?" I whisper.

"Not a chance." He shuts the door in my face.

Fair enough. I head to the greenhouse for some supplies, then back to our house. For the first time in twenty years, I've got some research to do.

I'M in the living room, deep in Mom's *Field Guide to Canadian Curses And How to Combat Them*, when Jasmine walks in, muttering under her breath about idiot sous chefs and yanking her black chef's coat off.

"Holy *shit!*" she screeches, holding a hand over her heart and heaving in a breath. "Where did you come from?"

I mark my place in the book and close it, leaning back onto the couch and eyeing her. "Been here the whole time."

She shakes her head, narrowing her eyes. "No…no. I always know when my sisters are in the house, and *where* they are in the house. And you…weren't there. Or, I guess, here," she says, waving her hand around.

I shrug. "Well, I'm here. Wanna tell me what's going on with idiot sous chefs?"

She shakes her head. "Absolutely not. Wanna tell *me* what's going on with Canadian curses?"

"Not yet."

She hums. "Can I make you something to eat?"

"You mean so you can get me to tell you everything when you put an intention into the food?" I scoff. "Not likely."

"I mean…maybe I'd do that," she says, unbraiding her long auburn hair and bending at the waist to shake it out. "Ahh, almost as good as taking off my bra," she sighs as she straightens. "In fact…" she trails off and proceeds to do exactly that, removing the pale pink cotton offender as though it's the cause of all her woes. Then she flops on the couch. "Much better."

I look down at the socked feet she's put in my lap. "Why are these here?"

"Because if you're not going to spill your secrets, then you're going to massage my feet. Consider it payment for scaring the daylights out of me earlier."

I grab a foot and get to work, remembering the massage Riggs gave me not that long ago. As Jasmine purrs with satisfaction, something occurs to me. "Hey, Jaz?"

"Hmm?"

"What did you mean when you said you know where we are in the house?"

"Ooh, harder on the arch—yes, bless your fucking soul."

She tosses her head back and bends an arm over her face. "Better than sex."

She mutters something else, but I don't catch it. "What?"

"Nothing," she answers.

"What about seeing us in the house?" I prod.

"Just something I've always been able to do. I can sense where each of you are, but only on our property."

"Not just the house?"

"Nope."

"Well, that explains why you always killed it at hide and seek," I grumble.

She laughs. "Yep."

As I rub her feet, the moans coming out of her sounding way more like sexual pleasure than I'd prefer, I try to recall when I last spent any quality time with Jasmine. And it hits me: not since before my Sixteenth Gathering.

I have a lot to make up for.

MAGNOLIA

AVA KNOWS SOMETHING'S up the instant she lays eyes on me in the parking lot on Monday morning. "Sweet hair," she says, gesturing at the streak, which is still plenty visible even though my hair is in its usual braids. "But something else is different. Did you bone him again?"

"I did not *bone* him," I say primly, but when I meet her eyes I snort a laugh. "Okay, maybe I did."

She holds her hand up for a high-five and pouts when I don't give it to her. Dropping her hand and adjusting the tote on her shoulder, she notes, "Got it. Not boning, but sex at least, no matter what you're calling it."

"Earth-shattering," I clarify.

She nods in his direction, where Riggs already stands greeting students. "Clearly."

I'd spent an hour last night talking to him like a teenager, too. When we finally clicked off, he said those three words to me, and I returned them, without hesitation.

"What's going on with the smile over there?" Ava asks

with a grin. "Looks like more than a boning situation. Do you like him?"

I look over at her. She's different, too. "You like the guy you're dating, don't you?"

Her face darkens with a blush. "I do, but we're talking about you. So spill it."

"So, the hair..." I start.

"Looks legit," she finishes. "Willow's skills are getting really good."

"It's because I told him I loved him."

"You *what*?!" she shrieks, and I swear everyone in the parking lot turns to look at us. She grabs both my arms and pulls my focus back to her. "You—you told him you loved him? Tell me he said it first. Please, god, tell me he—"

"He said it first." I laugh and extract myself from her grasp.

She heaves a sigh of relief. "Thank god, because I swear if you just let those three words rip..."

I shake my head. "When have I ever?"

"Oh, honey," she says, her brown eyes softening as she quiets. "You're really serious, aren't you? The two of you?"

I bite my lower lip. "We are. He's changing me, Ava. Like, *physically* changing me."

"Yeah he is," she laughs and leers at me. "Tell me more. What do you mean?"

"My magic. It's...back."

"I didn't know it was ever gone."

We start walking again, and after I give her the highlights of the weekend, she shakes her head. "Holy shit."

I chuckle. "That's one way to put it. The Gathering is coming up, and it's at our house this year, so I'm going to deal with it."

"How? You're gonna pull your sisters in, right?"

"Absolutely." I'm not ready, but I will be. "The thing is," I start, then hesitate. *Tell her. Be brave.* I adjust the tote on my shoulders and start again. "I've spent so long suppressing my magic that I have no idea what it really even is."

Ava makes a noise of agreement. "I don't remember you doing much with it before you were sixteen. Maybe I wasn't paying attention."

She's not wrong. "Mom preferred we contain our magic to the property until we turned sixteen," I answer. "Obviously, things went sideways for me."

Ava nods in agreement, and we stop the conversation because we're at the bottom of the steps. There, standing at the top and making my heart absolutely race, is Riggs. He quirks a smile at me, then goes back to paying attention to the students streaming past. An unreasonable spike of jealousy pings through me over every person he's looking at, and I want his eyes on me and only me.

Instantly he glances back, his eyes pinned to mine, heat and desire swirling through them.

"Jesus, did it get hotter out here?" Ava fans herself. "Riggs is looking at you like he wants to do unspeakable things."

I hold his gaze, feeling the power move within me. I let the unbridled want course through my body, let him see how much I need to feel his hands on my hips as he drives into me.

His hands clench and he turns to me, about to descend the stairs.

"Mags!" Ava hisses. "Whatever you're doing, *stop.*"

Her words land like a cold glass of water, and I shake my head to clear it. Sure enough, Riggs blinks and seems to refocus on the stream of students.

Crap.

As we ascend the stairs, Ava knocks me with her elbow. "Did you just...shit, I don't know what you just did."

"I think I need to talk to my mom."

"Good morning, Miss Green, Miss Rowan." Riggs hand reaches for mine.

I let our fingers brush together behind the cover of my legs. "Good morning, Principal Finlay." My voice is lower than I intend, and his eyes flare with heat once again. I read exactly what he'd like to do to me in his expression, and it involves his desk and me lying flat on it. There's no stopping the goosebumps that race over my body.

I manage to pull myself together, but from the minute that first bell rings, it's a long day of teaching. Normally, I love it. Chemistry can intimidate so many, but it shouldn't, and I love being the one to guide students through the confusion. Science is absolutely wondrous, beautiful even, and all you need to do is find the patterns and follow them. The chemicals, the way things mix or don't mix, the beauty of reactions beneath a microscope...nature will really show off for you if you bother to watch. And that's where it gets fun. Taking the time to watch, and question, and experiment.

But today? Today, I want to strangle almost every student. It's only the second week of school, so their bodies and brains haven't quite adapted back to the sleep and study schedule that's required, and it being a Monday makes it infinitely worse. No one's happy, least of all me, because I'm not concentrating, either. All I want to do is...well...Riggs. I want to feel his weight on top of me, his mouth on mine, as he peels my clothes off. I want the warmth of his skin against my own, the solid strength of his legs pushing mine apart as he enters me, burying himself to the hilt.

"Um, Miss Rowan?" Sunny speaks up, bringing me back to sixth period.

I blink and realize my entire classroom looks like it wants to, as Ava so delicately put it, bone. In one corner, the quarterback is looking at a flute player like he wants to eat her, and in another corner, two of the drama students have already pushed their desks together and I can't see their hands. Everyone is flushed. I can literally smell the pheromones.

This is much worse than I anticipated.

"Okay, class!" I exclaim, clapping my hands and attempting to bring order back to my own thoughts, and thus, my class's actions. I envision a cool winter breeze blowing in from the windows, and immediately sense a change in temperature and temperament. The quarterback blinks rapidly, seeming to come out of a trance, but the flute player might be irrevocably changed. And the drama kids don't bother putting their desks back to rights, but at least their hands are visible.

I'll call it a win.

And I have got to get control over myself and my thoughts.

Riggs

I HEAVE A sigh as I hang up the phone from the day's fourth angry-parent call about why their child deserves special treatment about this thing or the next. I knew this would happen, I really did. What I didn't expect was for it to be multiple calls per day, nearly every day. It's the second week of school, people. Second. Week.

God help me when report cards go out.

"Hey, Mrs. Hayes?" I call.

A moment later, the old woman's head pokes into my office. "Yes, Principal Finlay?"

"What's the vacation policy for principals? Think I can take two days off after every report card day?"

Her forehead wrinkles in confusion, then clears. "Ah, you're funny. No wonder you've got the whole town eyeballing you."

I snort. "Highly unlikely."

She looks at me over her thick glasses. "Principal Finlay. You are a charmer. You have muscles."

I choke. "Mrs. Hayes, I don't think—"

"Oh pfft," she interrupts. "I'm an old lady and I'll say what I want. You do know that the mayor is my niece, don't you? I assure you, she's well aware of my mouth. You know," she taps her chin, "she's single. Smart, too. As long as you're good with pant suits and an ungodly amount of cats?" She looks at me.

I blink.

She keeps looking at me.

"Oh." It finally sinks in. "You want me to—um, well, see…"

"Eh, you're not her type, now that I think about it," Mrs. Hayes says. "You know, you're lucky I've shielded you from the calls I get wanting to talk to you."

I pause, thinking of the litany I've waded through today. "From…parents?"

She raises a thin eyebrow. "Maybe you're not as smart as you look. Calls from *women*, Principal. Women. Who are interested in you, for themselves or their daughters."

Oh.

Listen, maybe I should have had "fend off interested single women" on my new-to-town Bingo card, but I didn't.

"Should I start forwarding those calls?"

"No!" I hurry to answer. "Sorry. Um, no. Definitely not."

She disappears.

"Mrs. Hayes?"

Her head pops back around the door. "Yes?"

"Thanks."

A genuine smile creases her face. "You're welcome, Principal Finlay."

"You ever going to call me Riggs?" I tease.

"Absolutely not," she responds, then disappears again.

My phone rings again, and I send it to voicemail. Why listen to another parent yell at me about their kid when I could think about the song I'll pick at karaoke tonight? Grabbing my cell, I open my music app and skim the playlist of my go-to songs.

I ALL BUT demanded Magnolia let me drive her to the bar this week, and she finally relented. And thank god, because I'm going out of my mind with the need to touch her, pull her close, bury my nose in her hair. And maybe, sure, bury something else into her...

I pull up to her house and see I'm easily a half hour early, so I head to the front door. I couldn't care less if she thinks I'm too eager—because I *am*. Eager to stop sneaking glances at her in the hallway, eager to do more than Face-Time her at night while she works on lessons or grades, eager to do more than sit next to her at the lunch table, surrounded by teenagers. Who knows? Since I'm here early, maybe I'll finally drink some of this legendary tea I keep hearing about. Or maybe I won't; Magnolia seems pretty adamant that I not drink anything unless she's the one handing it to me.

Voices rise as I near, and before I can even knock, the door is opening and Magnolia is there, her sweet scent wrapping around me as she tugs me inside.

"You're early," she murmurs against my neck as I hug her. "I'm sorry in advance."

I tilt my head. "What's—"

"Finally," comes Quinton's voice. "Maybe another mere mortal will bring some sense into this craziness."

I've stepped into...a very colorful, very chaotic situation. The energy in here is vastly different than last week when I showed up to take Magnolia on a date, and the fact that I'm suddenly commenting on the energy of a room is not lost on me.

Witches, man.

I recognize Magnolia's mom and Aspen from the apothecary, and neither one of them seem particularly calm. Willow flutters about like a hummingbird, and Magnolia stands to my left. On the blue velvet couch lays Clementine, with her head in Quinton's lap, a washcloth on her forehead.

"Are you insinuating that *men* are the only ones able to be sensible?" Clementine growls from the couch.

"I am not saying that," Quinton responds in what I bet he thinks is a soothing tone. It's not, but he's not looking at me to see the way I'm waggling my eyebrows to tell him to shut his mouth, for the love of god.

"Quit talking to me like I am a child!" Clementine snaps. "I'm a scientist, and just because you showed up doesn't mean I'm incapable of handling myself."

I can't take it anymore. Bro code and all that. "What's going on?" I ask blandly.

Clementine waves a hand. "I'm *fine*." She looks at everyone else as she speaks. "I swear, I'm fine. I just—"

"She fainted," Quinton interrupts.

I pull air between my teeth, and all I can think is, *Quinton, dude. Shut up.*

"It was barely—" Clementine starts.

"She was in the other room, and I heard her fall, and I lost my shit," Quinton steamrolls over her. "Does she let me take her to the doctor, like a normal person? Of course not. She demands I bring her here and threatens—"

"Promises," Clementine corrects.

"*Promises* if I don't that she'll put some kind of spell on me, and I swear to god, all of you witches are going to put me in an early grave."

Clementine rolls her eyes and tries to sit up. "Honestly."

"Lay down, woman," Quinton says, pushing her back down.

"We're not witches," she mutters.

We all snort. Even *I* know she's delusional if she thinks that.

"Keep telling yourself that." One of the twins—Juniper or Jasmine, I don't know which one—says, bringing her a cup of tea. "Mom's special brew."

"Can I sit up now, perfume prince?" Clementine asks Quinton.

"I hate it when you call me that," he mumbles.

"Yeah, well, *I* hate it when you go all alpha on me, so we're even." She sits up and glares at him, then accepts the tea from her sister, bringing it to her nose for a healthy smell or two before drinking.

"Just drink it," the twin says.

"I'm not about to let you pull one over on me just because I fainted," Clementine retorts.

Their mom crosses her arms as she leans in the doorway. "It's just tea. But honestly. You *did* come here instead of a hospital. What did you think would happen? We'd just let you go about your day?"

Clementine doesn't answer, and her cheeks flush as she takes her first sip of the tea. "Ooh, Mom. This is really good."

"Of course it is," the older woman responds as her thoughtful gaze lands on me. "I know what all my daughters need."

I stand up straighter, achingly aware that I'm the only person who isn't family in this room. Even Quinton is at least family by marriage.

"Where's Jasmine?" Clementine asks. "She's the only one not here."

Ah. That means the twin I'm looking at is Juniper.

"Hazel isn't here," Aspen says.

one and cross their arms. "Okay, okay," I give in. "Winner gets to pick their victory song."

"*And* picks the loser's songs for a month," Carol adds.

I whistle. "Damn, Carol. That's brutal."

Carol takes the high-five Seven gives her. "Not like either of you can't sing whatever you want. The both of you are ridiculous. Now shoo. I'm gonna get this thing going." She grabs a mic and flips the lights on, turning the corner into its own little disco party. "Okay, Al's, who's ready to sing?" The crowd claps, and she turns on Kelly Clarkson's *Since You Been Gone*.

"The real ridiculous person is Carol," I note as we head to the bar.

Seven hums in agreement. "Buy me a drink, handsome?"

"With pleasure." We get our standard — a beer for me, a whiskey neat with water on the side for her — and settle in for the night.

After three songs that weren't bad but weren't great, Seven leans against me the way she did at her house. "I can't believe we're here. Like this."

I take her in. The thick, wavy blonde hair that I now know she unbraids and brushes out to make it look that way. The bit of makeup that manages to make her look so vastly different from the high school chemistry teacher I looked at just a few hours ago. The streak of silver in her hair that we haven't talked about, that I know showed up the same night we traded I love yous. I lean down and coast my lips over hers, tasting the whiskey. "I can."

Her eyes search mine, looking for something. And I don't know if she finds it, because Carol is calling our names up and breaking down the rules for the crowd.

"You ready to eat my dust?" Seven puts her drink down and saunters to the stage.

I tug her back to me, putting my mouth at her ear. "Ready to eat something," I growl.

She cackles, then pirouettes away from me once more. When we get to Carol, she asks who's going first. "Me." Seven holds her hand out for the mic.

Carol hits play, and as the unmistakable sounds of the BeeGee's "Stayin' Alive" come out of the speakers, the smile that crosses Seven's face is absolutely feral. The crowd hollers, and Seven glides onto the riser, dropping into the seventies groove in two seconds flat. My glorious, witchy woman utterly slays it.

She sings the lyrics in a perfect falsetto, her eyes shining as the bar sings along with her. She grabs a woman to get up and do some of John Travolta's classic moves from the movie, and more join her. Everyone is dancing and singing, and Seven's got the whole place helping with the chorus so she can take the runs that Barry Gibb kills on the track, and the energy in the air is absolutely electric. By the time the song's over, I figure I'm beat.

Before the crowd's enthusiasm wanes, Carol goes straight to my song, Maroon 5's "Moves Like Jagger."

Seven's eyes narrow as she smiles and hands over the mic as I step up. The temptation to rip off my shirt is legitimately —and concerningly—strong, but I ignore it and start singing. The lyrics kick in quickly, and I know, without question, what Carol's going to do next.

And honestly? God bless her.

I start singing, hamming it up for the crowd. The full bar is watching now, so I give them…well, the moves like Jagger, and sing as much.

I keep going as Carol gestures for Seven off to the side, then slips her the other mic. I turn to Seven and curl my finger in a *come hither* move, and she slinks up next to me just in time for Christina Aguilera's portion. She sings right to me, crooning that I have to keep her secret if she shares it, and the words hit me entirely differently than ever before. She sounds almost exactly like Christina, the chameleon that she is, and she kills it.

I step close, running my hand over her waist before my part comes up, and then we duet, dancing and singing with each other. I've never been happier, and as we take the song to its conclusion, all I can think is how much I love her.

The song ends, but Carol isn't done. She nods at Seven and hits the next song.

I laugh and keep the mic. This is Seven's song, but it's possible that I have more lyrics than she does. I'm Wyclef Jean, and Seven is Shakira, because "Hips Don't Lie" swings into gear.

Seven's eyes go wide, beads of sweat starting to form on her forehead, and I lean into her. "You got this?"

She scoffs. "Hope you know Spanish."

"I know the Spanish in this song," I shoot back. Sort of. I'm going to mangle the shit out of it, and hopefully that won't count against me. I step up and start the rap, not caring that I have to look at the screen to make sure I've got the lyrics right.

Seven laughs into her mic, and during a break in the lyrics, asks the crowd if I should be dinged for having to rely on the screen.

Yeah, I don't care. I'll do whatever this woman wants. Especially as she starts to dance like fucking Shakira.

I. Am. Dead.

I can't decide whether Carol's a genius or if she's simply been waiting to spring this back-and-forth on us for a year. Probably both.

I swing up for a half-English, half-Spanish portion, singing about her dancing and what it makes me want to do.

And there's Seven, singing at me to read the signs of her body and for us to go slow.

Yeah, that might be a problem. She's swinging her hips side to side, singing in fucking Spanish like a champion, her blonde hair swinging across her body, strands of hair sticking to her face as she sweats, and all I can think is how I want that body sweaty above me.

I completely mangle the last portion of the song, and I don't give a shit. All I want to do is take Seven outside and lick her.

Carol isn't done. She puts Nelly's "Hot in Herre" on next, and a laugh gusts out of me as I put my hands on my knees. Still bent over, I put the mic up to my mouth. "Really, Carol?"

Seven chuckles into the mic. "Let's go, big boy. Nelly's calling."

Carol waves a bottle of water at me with the biggest smile I have ever seen, so I straighten and start singing as the lyrics kick in. "Want a little bit ah...and a little bit ah..." I grab the bottle, chug half of it, and swing around to point it at Seven, who knows good and damn well she's got a part to sing in this song. *Here we go. Thank god for down time in the Marines.* "I was like, good gracious..." and I'm off like a shot.

When it's Seven's time, she coos at me about wanting to take her clothes off while shaking that gorgeous ass at me. I'm losing my breath, and it's all her fault. I have to look at the screen for the last main push, because I have totally forgotten this song in the face of Seven writhing in front of me.

And damn if she doesn't take over, spitting the last section like a pro, and my jaw drops.

So what do I do? Obviously I sing the chorus again, hitting my own falsetto and crooning about taking my clothes off.

The crowd has lost its mind at this point, and Seven and I are grinning like fools. When the song finally ends, I'm certain we're done.

We. Are. Not. Done.

Carol moves to the next one, and it's "Hollaback Girl" by Gwen Stefani. Seven wilts for half a second, and all I can think is *thank fuck*. I get a break.

Like the clear champion she is, Seven morphs right into Gwen, her spine straightening while she sways back and stomps her feet, waving her arms to get the crowd to go with her. She sings into the mic and gives me a glance, and I confirm. I know what she wants without her asking, and I will be this woman's back-up singer until the end of time.

She lets us all know she's not a hollaback girl, and I pull my mic up to sing along with the crowd: "Ooh, this my shit, this my shit." When it's time to spell bananas, we even get Carol and the bartender going with us.

Carol finally takes pity on us when the song ends, stepping onto the small stage with more water for the two of us and addressing the crowd. "Okay, folks, time to choose our winner!"

Surprising no one, Seven takes it. She giggles and squeals, jumping into my arms and giving me a kiss in front of everyone. And as she presses into me, I don't care about the loss. I'm too busy enjoying the press of her body against mine.

Magnolia

F OR THE FIRST time in my life, I'm scared to go in the apothecary shop.

A woman walks up and stares at me expectantly, and I realize I'm blocking the door. Jerking into motion, I open the door and gesture her inside, then follow, confident that Mom is waiting for me. She always knows when I need her, and even though I've needed to talk to her for a week, it's taken me this long to finally get up the nerve to do it.

The bell above the door chimes as we walk in, like it always does, and as I look up, lavender tendrils of sound flow out of the metal.

I startle. That's...new.

A hand touches my arm and I jump.

"Whoa there," Aspen chuckles. "Nervous this morning? Need some tea?"

I narrow my eyes at her. "Depends on who's making it."

Her mouth tips up in a secretive smile. "You're looking for Mom."

"She in the back?"

"She is," Aspen confirms, then tilts her head. "What are you up to?"

"A lot. Actually, I need your help, too. Is Catherine working this morning?" I ask, referencing the high schooler who works after school and on the weekends.

In answer, Aspen threads her skinny arm through mine and we head to the back.

"How's Riggs?" Aspen asks conversationally.

I whip my head to her, unsure what to make of her inquiry. "He's...fine?"

"Good. I like him. He's...how to put it..." she muses, her steps slowing. Finally, she nods. "Good. He's good."

He's *good* all right. Good with his tongue and hands and other body parts, all of which I'd experienced several hours' worth of last night. It's a wonder I made it through school today. The one bonus of being so tired was that my magic seemed to be sleepy as well—no random horny teenagers thanks to my misplaced daydreaming.

Aspen grins. "Where'd you go, little sis?"

I blush. "Sorry. Yeah. Yes. I mean yes, he is. Good. Very good."

"Is he, now?" She smirks, then pulls me tighter against her and picks up the pace.

When we get to the tiny stockroom in the back, we find Mom on a stool, stretching to pull a box from a shelf that is way too high for her to reach. She doesn't bother turning around as she says, "Well, don't just stand there watching me. Come help."

"I don't know why you don't just move it," Aspen mutters, waving her hand at the box.

The box shifts forward, and Mom grabs it. Turning and stepping off the stool, she purses her lips at Aspen. "Because I prefer to use my magic at home only."

Aspen snorts derisively. "Sounds like a you problem."

Mom rolls her eyes. "I've lived long enough to know that some people are rather...*unnerved* by us. So I—"

"Hide," Aspen finishes. "Which I refuse to do."

It's an argument these two have frequently. Mom is only twenty years older than Aspen, and they bicker like sisters half the time. I think it's because they're so much alike. I'm only three years younger than Aspen, but she always gravitated toward Mom instead of me.

Then again, maybe that's my fault.

Mom opens the box. "We're waiting," she prompts, keeping her focus on her task. One after another, she pulls out dried spices in thick, flat plastic bags.

I can't get the words to come. Worrying my lip, I step around her to pull another box off the shelf, then turn to set it on the table next to her. I open it and inhale the star anise that wafts into the air, its licorice-tinted scent so powerful that no plastic can hold it back.

Seems I could take a lesson from the spice. Taking another inhale to gather my courage, I finally get the words out. "I need help."

Mom gives a soft hum. "I was wondering how long it'd take you."

I glance sharply at her. "How much do you know?"

She sighs. "Enough, but not everything."

I roll my eyes, already lighter at giving up the weight of the confession. "That is the most Mom answer you could possibly give."

Aspen laughs and agrees, "It really is." She sets a fresh box next to Mom and runs the scissors down the seam.

"Then start talking," Mom says. She trades Aspen for the new box and begins to unpack it, pulling out more bags of spices and herbs.

I breathe deeply, letting the familiar, yet muted, scents ground me. Bergamot, lavender, lemon, coriander...the list goes on and on. "I need help getting rid of a curse."

Mom stills.

"On who?" Aspen asks.

"Me."

The scissors clatter out of Mom's grip as Aspen's voice, sharp and acidic, cuts through the air. *"What?"* I swear spikes of dark yellow fly out of her mouth. Her whole body tenses, and I get the distinct impression that she is utterly and completely ready to kill someone on my behalf.

It's...oddly comforting.

"Kera cursed me at our Sixteenth Gathering."

Mom nods, as if that makes sense, and that tiny gesture seems to hold an entire world of explanation in it. A spike of heat, swift and sure, courses through me as I whirl on her, every instinct on high alert, and before I do something I will deeply regret, Aspen's hands are on my arms, pulling me tight against her chest. *What is happening?* Some base instinct screams to take her down, but I won't do it. She is my *mother*. It's only when Aspen has me fully wrapped in a bear hug, my back to her front, that I realizing I'm shaking uncontrollably.

"Shhh," Aspen soothes. "Hang on. Let her talk."

I *want* to calm down. I *want* to let Mom talk. I don't even understand my reaction right now, and all I can do is try to push it down as I breathe through it.

In front of me, Mom's eyes are wide, her hands held up as if...as if to fend me off? I shake my head, unable to fathom what my body is doing. Deep in my consciousness, something blinks awake and stretches.

"Mags? Are you okay now?" Aspen asks.

I grit my teeth and focus on my breathing. In for three counts, out for three counts. Aspen's arms squeeze harder. The parquet floor pops beneath us in the silence in the room. Finally, I manage to banish the urge to dominate, to control and punish, and I swallow thickly as the tension drains from my body. "I don't—" I look up at Mom, then choke out, "I don't know what just happened. I'm, god, I'm so sorry."

She holds her arms out and Aspen releases me. In two steps, I'm in my mother's arms, surrounded by her despite her tiny stature, and I crumple.

As she holds me, she speaks quietly. "I didn't know, Magnolia. I *did* know something happened. I couldn't put my finger on it, and after a couple of weeks, my memory around the Gathering got very fuzzy." She lets me out of her embrace and I sit on the stool, unable to make sense of, well, *anything.* She continues. "In fact, *you* got a little fuzzy, and stayed that way."

"Fuzzy?" Aspen and I say simultaneously.

"Fuzzy," she repeats. "Quite literally. You went out of focus to me. No one else noticed, of that I was certain, and I couldn't do anything to counter it."

I gape at her. "You're my *mother.* How could you not at least try?"

She walks to me and grabs my hands, looking up at me with her bright blue eyes. "My darling, we tried many, many times to counter it."

"We? There was no *we,*" Aspen says, her tone incredulous.

"Where was I in all this? You didn't think to loop me in?"

"Or me?" Aspen adds.

Mom looks at both of us. "You don't remember? Neither of you?"

I tense. "Remember what?"

Mom grips the table, her knuckles white with the effort of keeping her upright. "I did the spells with both of you. For two years. The three of us tried all manner of spells. Willow wasn't sixteen yet, and since she'd not had her Gathering, I knew she couldn't help. And obviously the others couldn't help—they were way too young."

The world spins around me. "This doesn't make sense. None of it."

"I think you both need to start at the beginning." Aspen's voice is strained. "Because neither of you are making any sense, and I'm about to lose my shit."

Sure enough, I look around and see that many of the boxes and jars around the room are vibrating, and some of them are close to tipping onto the floor. On instinct, I reverse the move she'd done to me only moments ago, closing the distance to Aspen and pulling her into a tight hug. She stiffens, her body taut and unfamiliar in my arms, but after a moment, she relaxes. "Thank you," she murmurs, her voice thick.

Eventually, I let her slip from my grasp. "I think it's *me* who should be thanking *you*." When was the last time we held each other? A memory floats into my consciousness, of us holding hands and running to Sacred River, the sun beating down on us, our feet bare and dirty, without a care in the world. It nearly knocks the wind out of me. I stare at her. "Aspen," I ask quietly. "Were we—Did we used to be close?"

Her brown eyes fill with tears instantly, and she looks up and away as she blinks them back.

My heart swells. "Oh god, Aspen. This is all my fault." I pull her to me once more. My prickly pear of a sister, who's never let anyone get close to her—was that because of me?

She squeezes my waist, which is all she can do because of how I've pinned her arms to her side in my embrace, and shushes me. "No, it's not."

"I think it might be." And I tell them what I found in my journal, about Kera's jealousy, her curse, my absolute despondency about it. My unwillingness to ask for help, which was utterly ridiculous in retrospect, and how I'd not bothered to look at my journal since I wrote my final intentions in it. And I tell them what those intentions were.

Mom and Aspen are quiet as I relay the story, their hands clasped against their chests. Mom seems to get more and more pale, while Aspen's porcelain complexion turns into an impressive shade of mottled red.

"That bitch," Aspen seethes. "Selfish, self-centered, egotistical, unworthy of being a witch...*bitch*."

Can't argue with her there. "I forgot that the journal existed, too. I mean, I'd see it, but it would immediately fall out of my head, if that makes sense?" They nod. "And it wasn't until—" I stop, trying to make it all make sense.

"Until what?" Aspen prods.

"Until Riggs. It wasn't until Riggs that things started...happening."

Mom hums thoughtfully. "When did you meet him—*really* meet him?"

I swallow. "Over a year ago. At karaoke."

Aspen looks at me quizzically. "Karaoke?"

"I hadn't gotten to that part yet. I have to sing or it makes me—"

"Sick," Mom finishes. "So that's what it's been all these years."

I nod. "I found I could go to this bar once a week and sing, and I'd be okay for a little while."

"You started getting clearer last year, when you met him," Mom says.

"Clearer? I've been out of focus to you this whole time?"

She gives me a sad smile. "I can almost see your eyes clearly again."

My heart breaks. "Oh, Mom."

Then I realize what she said—really realize. I started getting clearer *when I met Riggs*. And at that, it feels like the world grinds to a halt. "Wait."

And despite me holding my hand up, despite me not

wanting to hear what she's about to say, she says it anyway. "He's the one."

Magnolia

HE'S THE ONE.

Mom's words clang in my head like a gong in a canyon.

"What if that means—" I can't finish the statement. I can't even *think* it anymore. Not with the way my intentions and wishes seem to be shaping the world around me.

Aspen must realize it, too, because she reaches out to grab my arm, as though to stop me, and shakes her head. She looks back at our mom. "He's heard her sing."

Mom's lips tip up. "Oh, I think he's done more than that."

Heat rises to my cheeks at her words, but I don't bother denying it. Instead, I lay out the next piece of the puzzle. "I love him."

Aspen whistles. "I admit, I did not see it coming that fast."

"And it's just as terrifying admitting it to you two as it was telling him." I point to my hair. "This happened when I told him. He said it first, and after I said it, my head got all tingly. I saw it later."

"Love is a powerful thing," Mom intones.

Riggs

I'M GETTING USED to the controlled chaos of Magnolia's home. The splashes of color everywhere, the way the energy in the house ebbs and flows like a physical tide, shifting and rolling around me every time I enter. The tea.

Willow absolutely tried to get me earlier this week, handing me something that smelled closer to hot chocolate than tea. Right as I lifted it to my lips, mere seconds from taking a sip, Magnolia walked in and screeched.

I'd been so startled that I nearly dropped the cup and saucer to the hardwood floor, but managed to grip it tightly.

She'd pointed to Willow. "Are you seriously trying to give him Truth Tea?"

Her sister shrugged, wholly unapologetic. "I want to be sure he's worth all this."

Magnolia glared at her as she poured the tea down the sink. "He is."

I still wasn't sure what "all this" meant, but I was also getting used to not knowing everything. I figured it was best if I didn't, something that Ava had confirmed over lunch.

"They're witches, Riggs," she said. "You don't *want* to know all the things they're up to. Granted, it's weird that Mags is taking part, because she used to never take part. But —" she hesitated.

"But what?" I prompted.

"But she's changed. In a good way," she hurried to say. "So if she says whatever she's doing is important, then it's important."

I'd nodded and smiled like a good boy. Because that's what you do when you're a man and you're ninety percent certain you're supposed to understand what the woman in front of you is talking about.

Now that I've got three weeks of school under my belt it's time to see Pops. With Magnolia.

She opens the door before I can knock, another standard occurrence with the entire family. She leans in for a kiss, and like always, I want to stop time to get my fill: lush curves pressed against me, long, wavy hair tickling my hands, her green apple scent surrounding me. I tighten my grip around her waist, growling into the kiss as our tongues slide together. She whimpers, tipping up on her toes as her nails scratch the back of my neck.

In seconds, it feels like I'm standing on the surface of the sun while my insides boil. I break away from her, gasping for air and feeling more than a little sweat beading on my brow. "Um, babe?"

The rosy blush that stains her cheeks and neck is nothing short of spectacular. "Sorry. I'm trying to get that under control."

I laugh and pull her to me, resting my hand on the small of her back. The 'that' is how her emotions can influence just about everything around her: people *and* the environment. "I kind of like knowing that's the effect I have on you," I say.

She swats at me. "Yeah, well, tell that to my students."

I smirk. "I'm going to start docking your pay for all the broken beakers that have suddenly met their untimely death around you," I tease.

"Shut up."

"Hi Riggs," Willow calls as she walks to the front. She stops and gives Magnolia a big hug, and I watch as Magnolia melts into it. She's like a well-trained dog with touch. Craves it beyond belief, yet holds herself apart. Once you touch her —once you let her know you want to be touched and want to touch her—it's on.

"I'm heading to the shop," Willow continues. "Stop by for some tea blends on your way?" she teases, winking at me.

"You're incorrigible," Magnolia says. As Willow drifts past me, Magnolia hesitates.

"What is it?"

"Do I—do I look okay? I know it's silly to worry about it, but…" she trails off, her eyes sliding toward the ground.

"You're gorgeous. Always. And you look like a dream, Magnolia." I twirl her around so her new knee-length skirt, dark purple with polka dots, can flare around her. She's also in a dark purple T-shirt and cute white sneakers.

She smooths her hands over the skirt. "I wanted to try something different. So I raided my sisters' closets."

"You could have chosen a paper bag and Pops would still think you were a goddess," I say. "And he'd be right."

Pops won't let go of her hand. We've been here an hour and he's as enchanted by her as I am, sitting right next to her with hardly an inch separating them. I can't be upset about the moves he's making, though, because he looks so good.

Being here has done wonders for him. His eyes are bright and aware, his lined face is full of color. He's happier now than I've seen him in years, and I couldn't be more grateful. I wish I could have convinced him to move here sooner, but I shove that guilt down as Pops takes a drink of his lemonade and turns back to the woman of the hour.

"Tell me how you two met," he says, finally releasing her. He knows the story, but I don't interrupt as Magnolia speaks.

She smiles. "We met at karaoke. Surely he's told you."

Pops scoffs. "Of course he's told me, but he's a caveman. I'm lucky I got more than some grunts and a few sentences out of him."

"Is that right?" Magnolia laughs. "Well, he's a caveman with an amazing voice."

"That he is," Pops beams.

"Let's see, it was about a year and a half ago, right, Riggs?" She turns those whiskey eyes on me.

"I remember the song you sang."

Her eyes widen. "You do not."

I hold my hands up. "Honest truth, I absolutely do. You swept me off my feet with that voice."

She rolls her eyes. "Okay, Romeo. What was it?"

I smirk, because I absolutely have her on this one. "You did a back-to-back of Dolly Parton's '9 to 5' and Aretha Franklin's 'Respect.' There was no going back. How can I not fall in love with a woman who sings Dolly and Aretha, *and* sounds like them?"

Magnolia blushes, and Pops gives me an appraising look. "Smart man."

"Do you sing? Or did your wife?" Magnolia asks.

Pops shakes his head. "Not me, that's for sure. I'm the real caveman around here if we're talking about singing. My wife, on the other hand? Like an angel." His voice wobbles a little.

"Mom was a special woman." I catch his gaze and hold it.

"That she was."

The doorbell rings. "Expecting someone? One of your many lady friends?" I tease.

Pops waves me off. "None of them hold a candle to your mom."

I rise and walk to him, then kneel before him. "Of course they can't. And they're probably just as wonderful in their own ways. There's no reason you can't be happy and have company, you know."

"I do know, son." He smiles and pats my cheek. His hands feel different now, smooth, the calluses of years as a Marine and helming his own construction company worn away. His arms are smaller than I'd like, and the skin itself is different now, thin and mottled with age, but even still, the gesture is so typical of him that it makes my throat thicken.

"Well." I swallow roughly and rise. "I'll go get that."

MAGNOLIA

T'S NOT JUST one woman at the door. It's four. It's a Golden Girls episode come to life, and I am fairly certain I have never had more fun in my life. The women are hilarious, clearly having lost all manner of caring what anyone thinks and so comfortable with themselves and each other that there is truly no telling what will come out of their mouths.

Listening to them is fascinating. Wanda tells me of her husband Robert, who she met outside the radio station in 1939 in Yazoo, Mississippi, where he was a radio musician. Catherine's husband was a pilot in World War II while she worked on Liberty ships in Richmond, California. Sharon taught elementary school. Rosanna was a nurse, never married, and I catch on pretty quickly that she's not here for William.

The women stay for a short time, relatively speaking, before departing. "We didn't know you'd have visitors today!" Catherine says. "We'll see you later this week at bingo."

William walks the quartet to the door before disappearing

into his room for a moment. I look at Riggs. "You gonna be a ladies' man like that when you're old? Head full of hair, bright eyes, incorrigible flirt?"

Riggs chuckles and runs a hand through his hair. "I'm already a silver fox, babe. Guess we'll have to see if I outlive you," he teases.

I swat at him even as my heart squeezes at the promises embedded in his words. Does he mean them? The warmth in my chest burns hot at the thought of him and I growing old together, sitting on the porch and holding hands while we watch the sunset, followed quickly by the cold dread of the curse's threat.

When William comes back out, he shoos Riggs outside to "check the drainage pipes," which Riggs and I both know is completely ridiculous. He leaves anyway, and I prepare for what I assume is going to be a "my son is a wonderful man" speech.

"Riggs says you're a witch," William says without preamble.

Choking on air, my cheeks heat as my eyes widen.

The old man chuckles and hands me the glass of lemonade I'd been drinking. As I gather myself back together and take a sip, he continues, "You do a poor job of hiding your emotions, but I bet you know that."

I set the glass down and consider him. The woman I was a month ago would have lied. Now, I breathe through the sudden pounding of my heart. It shouldn't matter that his dad knows, and it doesn't. Not really. What's surprising is how worried I am that William won't want me around his son.

Exhaling, I try to channel some of Wanda, Catherine, Sharon, and Rosanna's energy. Their air of not caring, or at least not letting other people's emotions and feelings be something that they feel responsible for. "Yes, I am."

He smiles. "My grandmother was a witch."

The surprise rushes through me like a lightning bolt. "What? Really?"

William shrugs his bony shoulders. "Riggs doesn't know —hell, my own wife didn't know—but yes. She was my paternal grandmother, and she got what little magic she had from her father's side."

"Not very powerful, then," I surmise. A witch's power is determined by her mother, always. Men were only carriers of the magic, unable to wield in any capacity. So their offspring are always less powerful, unless they conceive with another witch. Magic is absolutely hereditary, and how strong one's magic is depends entirely on their bloodline.

"Correct. My dad, of course, had nothing. And Riggs and I have a whole bunch of nothing."

"Where was your grandmother from?"

"Louisiana."

I grin. "Old magic, then. You *sure* you're not carrying anything, William?"

He chuckles. "My grandmother's stories were always almost too fantastic to believe. Tales of wielding magic in the bayou, talking alligators, you name it, she wove a story about it. And believe me, I tried so hard to wield magic. Was convinced that I'd be the male to change the rule. Because why not?"

"And did you?" I ask, even though I know what the answer is going to be.

"Of course not. Was a real disappointment when I finally accepted it."

I reach over and pat his knee. "Happens all the time."

"Right."

"Why didn't you ever tell Riggs? It's not something to be ashamed of."

"This is going to sound terrible to you, but telling him

simply never seemed pertinent. No one talked about it in my family once my grandmother passed, so it seemed rather moot." He rubs his chin and goes quiet for a minute, his gaze unfocused. "Now that he's met you, it's time I told him."

My silly heart flops over, ridiculously happy at the news. I take another sip of my lemonade. "Well, maybe all this is why he was so accepting of me in the first place. He took it awfully well."

"Doesn't surprise me at all." He reaches into his pocket and pulls out a black velvet pouch. "My grandmother gave this to me before she died. Said one day I'd know exactly what to do with it. Meeting you, I finally do." He unties the pouch and pulls out a stone.

When he holds it out to me, I gasp. "Is that—"

"It is," William confirms, tilting the object toward me. "A veilstone."

Time seems to slow and warp. Beautifully simple in its resting form, the stone is round and nearly egg-shaped, milky-white yet almost translucent, with hints of faint rainbow-colored streaks darting through it. To the untrained eye, it looks like moonstone. Show it to a witch, and she'll know exactly what it is. Always.

"Do you know how few of them there are?" I say, still not reaching for it, even though I swear it's reaching for me, its energy pulsing steadily toward me.

"Take it."

I shake my head. "I—I can't. It's not my family's. I'm not even supposed to *touch* it."

William studies me, his eyes such a familiar blue that it's like looking at Riggs in three decades' time. "Do you know why my grandmother gave this to me?"

"There had to have been other witches in the family—"

"There weren't," he interrupts me. "She was the last, and

knew it. She was absolutely certain that I'd meet a witch worthy of receiving this stone."

"You don't understand," I insist. "Veilstones are precious. Tied to certain families and bloodlines. My family has never—"

"Magnolia," he says gently.

Rubbing my hands on my skirt, I focus on the polkadots and try to calm the way my body is reacting. Waves of terror and excitement take turns washing over me, and the combination is both heady and nauseating. I bend over and stick my head between my legs, murmuring, "Sorry. I don't feel very well."

"I understand. I still need to finish the story."

I take a few breaths, then sit back up. "What about Riggs?"

"Is legitimately doing things outside. He knows I had something for you, but doesn't know what. Now, can I finish?" His eyes sparkle with mischief.

I swallow, my gaze darting to the veilstone and back. It's mesmerizing, and the more I look at it, the more visible the energy pulsing around it becomes. A low hum of electricity begins to run through me. "Yes."

"My grandmother was adamant that I'd meet a witch. I admit, I was beginning to think she was full of it. Yet here I am, eighty years old, finally meeting you. She told me that the witch wouldn't be the love of my life but of someone else close to me. That her eyes would be the color of caramel and freshly turned earth, and that she would refuse the veilstone at first. But that it was imperative she receive it." He pauses. "You, my dear, are that witch."

I squeeze my eyes shut, unable to bear what's in front of me. How am I supposed to take this veilstone? I've never seen one in person. And to know that William has had one for decades, sitting in a velvet pouch just waiting on...on *me*, is knowledge I'm not sure I'm ready to accept.

Distantly, the front door opens and closes, and within moments I catch the cedar scent of Riggs. I feel his hands on my shoulders, heavy and sturdy, and the touch grounds me. Reminds me that taking something this powerful isn't about me. It's about my family. About Riggs, and even William. I owe it to the Universe—no, to *myself*—to take it. If I am to step into the power I know I possess, then I can't shun the gifts that are quite literally in front of my face. Besides, it's a veilstone, and who says no to a veilstone? No one.

Resigned, I open my eyes. "Okay."

William beams. "Good." He extends his hand, offering the veilstone to me.

"Could you—" I hesitate. The scared part of me wants to ask William to put it back in its velvet bag, and then have Riggs carry it until I can get back to my house and family. Every other part of me knows I need to accept it from him, or the veilstone won't recognize me as its new owner. "Can we stand?"

Riggs comes around to help his father stand, looking between the two of us with about a hundred questions written on his face. "I'm good with whatever is happening here," he says, "but I'd really love to have a clue before something happens."

William huffs out a dry laugh. "It's a long story, son."

"I'd still like to know," Riggs insists as William straightens and keeps his hold on Riggs.

"Your great-grandmother was a witch, the last in our family. She entrusted me with a magical stone and told me to give it to Magnolia."

Riggs's eyes widen. "We've got witches in our family?"

"Not anymore. Magnolia can explain it later." William

chuckles at the expression on his son's face. "I'm getting tired, and I'd really like to give this stone to your girlfriend."

Riggs turns to me, his gaze serious. "Are you okay?"

I shake my arms out. "I will be. This is…" I struggle to put it into words, so I finally go with, "This is a really big deal. What your father is giving to me is very rare, and likely very powerful."

With his free hand, Riggs reaches for mine and squeezes it. "I believe in you, Magnolia. You've got this."

I blink back the sudden emotion that swells in my throat and threatens tears. His words are simple, but they mean so much. "Thank you."

"So will you just take the damn rock already?" William asks.

I burst out laughing. "No," I smile and look around. "I really do need to get into the right headspace. Gather around the coffee table. William, put the veilstone in the middle of the table. Let's all hold hands."

Riggs wiggles his eyebrows. "Ooh, do we get to be a part of a ritual?"

I roll my eyes. "No. No men allowed, remember?" I tease.

"Really sexist, don't you think, Pops? No warlocks to speak of?"

I make a face. "Warlocks aren't even a thing."

"Mages? Wizards? Sorcerers?"

"You're reaching. Women only. Sorry, babe," I laugh as I watch his face fall. "Look," I soothe. "This isn't a ritual, but it's important and you're helping."

That seems to make him feel better. We all clasp hands as I close my eyes, inhaling and exhaling deeply. I pull all my focus, all my intention, into the room, envisioning the three of us forming a circle of light around the veilstone, wrapping the stone in layers of protection and woven with rays of sunlight and moonlight. I feel the warm, strong grip of Riggs on my right, and the dry, lighter touch of William to my left. My chest warms with energy, and I breathe deeper to welcome it. I'm acting on pure instinct now, and I let the Universe take over.

The temperature in the room rises and a small wind blows. No one speaks, and when I open my eyes, my gaze goes straight to the veilstone.

The pale, milky-white stone glows like the full harvest moon, a corona of light pushing out from it, pulsing with energy.

My voice is low when I speak. "William, please take the veilstone in your left hand."

The old man obeys, his grip on my hand growing tight as he uses me for balance. As he picks up the stone, he gasps. "It's hot," he says, his voice full of wonder.

"William, what was your grandmother's name?"

"Eugenia Aryton," he answers.

The light around the veilstone pulses, sending out a rainbow of energy that broadens and expands, filling the circle before moving through us and disappearing.

"Whoa," Riggs whispers.

I send a thank you to Eugenia and feel an answering wind in response. She's here with us, having left a part of herself in the stone like all those to have possessed it before her, but I know to keep that part to myself. I turn my attention back to William, who stares at the veilstone in silent awe.

"Am I the witch you wish to give this veilstone to?"

He jerks his attention to me and nods gravely.

My lips tip up. "I think you should say it out loud."

William clears his throat. "Y-yes. I, William Finlay, wish to give you this veilstone, which I have kept safe at my grand-mother Eugenia Aryton's request. It is yours."

I can't help my smile at his effort to be so formal. "Thank you."

Riggs squeezes my hand, and I look at him. He is surrounded by a deep red and orange aura, and it has nothing to do with the veilstone. Wordlessly he mouths, *"I love you."*

The love that swells in my heart is almost too much, and it nearly overtakes me. *"I love you, too,"* I mouth back. Gulping air, I force myself to focus back on transferring the veilstone. "Ready?" I ask William.

"I am."

Keeping my left hand clasped with William's, I release Riggs and hold my hand out for the stone. He places it in my palm.

A crack of energy pulses in the room, sending a miniature lightning bolt through the air between us.

"Holy shit," Riggs yelps.

I don't pay him any attention. I can't. I'm being electrocuted. Energy crackles through me, sending spikes of flaming heat down my arms and legs and into my fingers and toes. My head tingles as I fight to keep my attention on the veilstone as it pulls all the light from the room into it. Shadows darken the surrounding space, and all I can do is let the veilstone continue. Light pours into the rock, heating it and my palm to an almost unbearable temperature. I maintain my hold, and in moments, the room goes utterly dark.

A millisecond later, bright light shoots out of the veilstone, pulsing in wave after rainbow-hued wave as it expands out and around us, bathing the room in a warm glow before dissipating and leaving the room as it was. Inside my palm, the now-cooled stone rests. I lift it higher for inspection, and there, moving through the center among the translucent lines of rainbow, is a new line of bright white.

I lay her down and unlace her shoes, pulling them and her socks off.

"What are you doing?" Her voice trembles with the question.

I pull my shirt off. "Making you forget," I answer, not missing the way her eyes fall to my chest. "Will you let me do that for you?"

She hesitates, so I undo my jeans and push the flaps open, knowing good and damn well that it distracts her. When she pulls her bottom lip between her teeth, I know I've won. "Okay," she whispers.

I pull her shirt off, then her bra, followed by her skirt and panties. I shuck everything off and step out of my shoes. Once I have the both of us naked, I walk away.

She chokes out a strangled noise behind me. "Where are you going?"

"To start the shower. It's a great shower."

It really is. It's a walk-in with two shower heads, one on either side, and there's a built-in seat on one side that's perfect for a certain someone to relax while I go down on her.

"You should come with me," I call over my shoulder. Sure enough, by the time I've started the shower, turning on both heads and stepping out to let the water heat up, she's in the bathroom. "Want your hair up?"

She tips the corner of her lips up. "You really think it's going to stay dry?"

Caught, I laugh. "Probably not, but I figured it was worth the offer."

She presses her forearms against my chest, sending that familiar spark into me, and I groan as her lips meet mine. She hums, then stops and pulls away.

"Mags," I murmur. "It's okay."

Worry fills her eyes. "You don't know that."

"I know that you humming surely isn't going to be the

death of me. Come on." I gently pull her into the shower and guide her under the spray. She closes her eyes and I take a moment to appreciate the view. Generous breasts and curves, a rounded belly and hips perfect for grabbing onto, and that fucking bare pussy.

Jesus.

I sink to my knees without a second thought, needing my mouth on her immediately. She gasps and grabs onto my shoulders for balance as I part her lips and lick.

"Riggs," she breathes. "I can't…"

"You can."

She shakes her head. "I need…"

"Please," I interrupt. "Let me make you feel good." I wait, my knees on the tile and my hands on my thighs.

She inhales shakily, then closes her eyes. "Okay."

Grateful she's consented, I turn my attention back to her beautiful pussy. As I dip my tongue between her once more, I groan with hunger. I want this every day. Want to taste her, feel the way she melts around me, hear the way her voice goes to this particular smoky timbre only when I'm bringing her pleasure. Because my god, this woman.

I manage to pull myself from her long enough to growl at her to sit on the tiled seat, then move toward her. I pull one of her nipples into my mouth, swirling and nipping at it the way she likes, and feel her hands push through the buzz of my hair.

"Fuck," her voice hitches. "That's so good."

I release her nipple, licking up her chest to her neck and the sensitive shell of her ear. "Tell me what you want, Magnolia," I urge, palming and squeezing one of her breasts tightly.

She jerks. "More."

"More what?"

"Put your mouth on my pussy, Riggs. Make me come."

My cock thickens almost painfully as I growl against her

neck. I fucking love it when she talks like that. "Good girl, Magnolia." I pump my cock once for relief, then descend, pulling her foot up on the seat and pushing her knee wide, baring her to me. "God." I stare, pumping myself again.

"Riggs." She wiggles and moves a hand near her clit.

I raise an eyebrow at her. "Change of plans."

She heaves a breath and looks at me with glassy eyes.

"Touch yourself," I demand.

"Only if you do," she responds.

I don't answer. Instead, I wrap my hand around the base of my cock and give it a long, slow stroke.

"Is that how you like it?" she asks, dipping a hand between her legs and beginning to swirl her middle finger around her clit.

I nod, transfixed on her hand, the way her fingers are bent, the angle of them against her pink flesh. "Don't stop doing that."

She shifts a little, but keeps her legs spread for me, and keeps circling her clit, up and down. I grip myself harder, worried I'll come way too fast at the rate we're going.

"Talk to me," she whispers, her voice barely audible over the shower.

"You're so fucking gorgeous," I choke out. "I've wanted you from the minute I saw you singing, and *fuck*." I trail off as she pushes that same middle finger into herself, then a second finger, using her thumb to stroke her clit. "Baby."

"Does it feel good?" Her gaze meets mine. "Fisting yourself? Fucking your hand?"

Holy shit. I grip myself harder and move faster as my breath comes in short, choppy bursts. "Yes. Fuck, yes. You?"

She arches her back and moans. "You're so sexy, Riggs. Watching you." She pumps her fingers in and out, circling her hips and writhing on the bench.

I can't say anything, simply hope that I can hold off long enough to watch her take herself to the brink.

Holding my gaze, she says, "I can't wait to have your cock inside me. Filling me. Spilling into me."

"*Fuck*, Magnolia," I growl, nearly out of my head. I use my free hand to brace myself against the tile, dangerously close to passing out from pleasure.

"Riggs. I'm almost there," she pants.

"Look at me," I plead, feeling my own release build.

She locks eyes with me as she cries out with her climax, and I let myself go, the heat of the water nearly my undoing as my vision narrows with the intensity of my own orgasm. Braced against the tile for support, I open my eyes to see Magnolia, gloriously undone on the seat in front of me. As she pulls her hand away from herself, I step forward, grabbing her wrist and guiding her fingers to my mouth. Her eyes darken, then flutter with desire as I suck them into my mouth, tasting her release on my tongue.

Not even remotely satisfied, I kneel before her, intent on finishing the task I'd begun.

"Riggs, I can't—" she starts.

I ignore her, dipping my tongue into her wet heat before swirling it back out and around her swollen clit. "You taste so fucking good." Her hips jerk in response, and she grabs the hair on top of my head. "There you go," I mutter, then suck her clit into my mouth, flicking it with my tongue and pushing two fingers into her without warning.

Water beats down on my back as I take her, curling my fingers inside her to find the spot that sends her soaring.

"Fuck, fuck, fuck," she chants above me, then stiffens. I pump harder, and flutter my tongue just below her clit, on the spot I've found is her most sensitive.

She screams, the sound echoing beautifully, and I half expect the panes of the shower glass to crack in response. As she goes nearly boneless in the aftermath, I straighten, hiding the wince of pain that kneeling on the tile with fifty-year-old knees brings.

She pulls herself upright, palms on either side of her, and blinks up at me.

I smile. "Now that's the kind of blissed-out face a guy loves to see." She blushes as I turn to get some things to wash her with.

After we're done washing, I pull her out and wrap her in a towel, then squeeze the water from her hair. "Do you want to dry it?"

She looks at me quizzically. "With what?"

I open the sink cabinet and point to the hair dryer that still sits in its box from where I bought it a week ago.

"That's sweet," she coos.

"I know," I chuckle, then duck the swat she tries to give me.

"Don't be so egotistical."

"I know what I'm good at." I step behind her and kiss the skin between her neck and shoulder. She makes a sound of contentment, then squeals as I spank her ass. "Dry your hair. I know you don't want to come to bed with it wet."

"Who says I'm going to bed?"

"Me," I answer, kissing her skin again.

I notice she doesn't argue when I leave her to it.

She also doesn't argue when I pull her into the bed and put my head between her legs again. Or when I push into her, groaning her name as she tightens around me. Her arms are banded around me, and we move together in the dimness of twilight, our breathing in sync.

"I love you," she whispers against my skin.

I pull her mouth to mine as our hips meet again and again. "I love you, too, Magnolia."

"And I'll kick your ass if I have another streak in my hair after I come."

I thrust hard into her and smirk as her eyes flare. "You're saying it won't be worth it?" I push again.

She moans and her eyes flutter shut. "Keep doing that and I won't care."

I'm happy to say that when she comes, her mouth fused to mine in a kiss so deep I nearly lose my breath, she does *not* get another streak of silver in her hair.

Magnolia

T DREAMED IT was my first day of school as a teacher. Except I wasn't prepared for anything, and instead of teaching chemistry, I was teaching English Literature. And all the kids were bored, and they hated me, and we didn't have any desks. Then we were flying kites, except we didn't have any string, and the football players were calling plays with the kites and the cheerleaders were zombies.

Basically, the stress dream to end all stress dreams. Zero out of ten, do not recommend.

What I *do* recommend, however, is waking up in a sexy man's bed, with said sexy man then immediately dipping his fingers into you, swirling them around and making you come so hard you see stars.

It's enough to make me think I need to seriously consider waking up with him more often.

But it's Sunday, and ever since I can remember, Sundays have been reserved for all of us sisters to make our way to the house for a day of magical whatever, followed by dinner. Sometimes it's as easy as gathering up the gems and crystals and stones and charging them in the sun while we lay in the shade of the willow tree. Other times—okay, *most* of the time —it's a bit more intense. Things like pulling together all the Tarot cards that Mom leaves lying around the house and cleansing them with a sage rub ceremony, or pulling out the scrying bowls and washing them with a mix of olive and lavender oil. This time, it's a whole different ball game.

The veilstone practically hums as I pull onto the driveway, and the velvet carrying pouch is warm to the touch as I gather it up to take it inside. I have no doubt it can sense the magic of the surrounding land, and maybe the various gifts that each of my sisters have. I near the door and it opens without me touching it, and when no one appears on the other side, the expectant smile on my face falls.

What the hell?

My pulse kicks up as worst-case scenarios begin swirling through my head. The Universe is punishing me for being gifted the veilstone. Something's happened to Clementine and the twins. Hazel's been hurt and everyone went to Boston. There was a fire at the apothecary when William handed the veilstone over to me. There—

"Magnolia? What are you doing?"

Aspen's voice yanks me back to earth, and I exhale as I look at her. "Is everything okay?"

Two thin lines appear between her eyebrows. "Of course. Is everything okay with you?"

I open my mouth to speak, but can't find the words. Finally, I say, "Um, yes?"

She peers at me as though she's waiting for a mole to crop up on my nose.

"The door—it opened for me?" I don't know why every-thing that's coming out of my mouth is in the form of a question.

Aspen's face smooths. "Is that all?"

"It's never done that for me."

She gives a noncommittal shrug. "It's a thing."

"Since when?"

"Since your magic is getting stronger. The door only opens for Mom, and now you. It opened for me a few times around a full moon in my twenties, but then I accidentally spilled some bleach on the threshold when I was cleaning, and I don't think the house has forgiven me."

I nod dumbly. How did I not know that the house did that for Mom?

Aspen tilts her head. "Come on. We're all here. In the back, under the tree. Mom thought I'd be the best one to wait on you." She holds her hand out, and I stare at it for a minute before realizing she wants me to take it.

I don't remember the last time I held one of my sisters' hands. Emotion clogs my throat as I take her hand and follow her through the hall, into the kitchen, and out of the kitchen door to the deck. A pair of cardinals chirp in the small pear tree that Clementine plans to put into the ground next year, and I whistle at the birds without thinking. They call back to me, and Aspen chuckles.

"Haven't heard you do that in a long time," she says, a fond smile on her face. "I've missed it. I've missed *you*."

I squeeze her hand. "I'm back," I promise her. "And I'm not going anywhere."

We approach the willow tree, and everyone is there: Mom, Willow, Juniper, Jasmine, and Clementine. We're a wild bunch to look at, none of us really resembling each other except for the twins.

Mom, looking like a mythical pixie with her four-foot-four self and short, gray hair with ears that I swear seem just the *teensiest* bit pointed. Willow, the most otherworldly-looking of us all, with her hair more white than blonde, wide-set amber eyes, and Mediterranean skin. Aspen, the tallest and thinnest of us all, with thick blonde hair so dark it's more brown than

anything, and caramel, almond-shaped eyes that tilt up a
smidge. The twins, both with dark auburn hair waving down
their backs and skin so freckled they look tan, and hazel eyes
that shift with their mood. Clementine, who very much looks
like a cartoon fairy gone slightly wrong, with moss green eyes
and black hair that's usually knotted with a pencil on top of
her head. Even seated, she's already showing, her tiny belly
already rounded and adorable in a way that makes me both
fiercely protective and oddly nostalgic.

Now that I've gotten all my memories back, I realize that
Sundays were really the only quality time I ever spent with
my sisters. My heart aches to think of what I've missed:
secrets and crushes and the everyday highs and lows of their
lives. I know my sisters, but I suspect it's much more surface
level thanks to my stupid self asking the Universe to keep
them away from me and safe.

Before anyone can speak, I hold up the velvet pouch. "I
have news."

"HOLY *shit!*" Jasmine's eyes are wide as she covers her
mouth with both hands. Green sparkly light shoots out from
her aura, a mixture of fear and excitement.

Even Clem is silent, not admonishing Jasmine for the
curse, her normally bright orange aura now a deep, burnt
umber.

Aspen is deadly still, her pale gray aura hugging her close,
and even Mom doesn't seem to know what to do with herself.
They're all staring at the veilstone as it rests in my palm.

"It looks like moonstone." Willow leans closer.

"Can't you feel it?" Juniper asks.

"I feel something," Willow answers. "How do I know it's this stone?"

"It's the stone," I assure her. "It seems pretty happy to be here, even though none of you seem to know how to react."

"Wait." Jasmine finally peels her gaze off the stone and looks at me. "Are you telling me that rock has emotions?"

My hand spasms as the stone releases a spark of annoyance into me, and for some reason I can't explain, the whole thing makes me laugh. "Yeah, it definitely has emotions, and I don't think it liked you referring to it as a rock." A beat passes. "Am I the only one here who knows about veilstones?"

Everyone shakes their head, and Clementine says, "I think we're all just processing. You're *sure* it's…yours?" she asks. "And I don't mean that in a mean way. I guess I'm just trying to be certain that you truly were gifted the stone—"

"Or we're all up a creek," Aspen finishes.

"I get it. William's grandmother Eugenia Aryton was the last witch in her line. She told William he'd meet me. Well, not *me* specifically, but me nonetheless. Besides," I give them a wry smile, "it gifted me this new streak." I point to my hair.

"Told you it wasn't dye," Juniper mutters to Jasmine, who pokes her back.

"Ow!"

"Girls!" Mom finally comes to her senses. "Yes, it's definitely a veilstone and yes, it's definitely Magnolia's. See that white vein going through it?" She points to the fissure running through the stone. "That happened when William gave it to you, didn't it?"

"Yes," I confirm.

Mom nods decisively. "This changes things. I'd planned on one way to attack Kera's curse, only now that you have the veilstone…" she trails off. "I think we need to do a little more research."

"How would the veilstone help?" Jasmine asks.

"It depends," Mom answers. "Every veilstone is different, because it's guided not only by the one who possesses it, but by the spirits of those who went before them. I don't know anything about the Aryton witches, but perhaps that will help us better understand it." Mom looks at me. "Did William tell you what he did with it all these years? How he stored it?"

I shrug. "I have a feeling it's been in his sock drawer for decades." When the stone sends a confirmation pulse into my hand, I squeeze it in return. I feel a little bad that I left it sitting in the dark in my purse overnight, so I look at it and promise to give it a lovely altar soon.

"Okay, but can we talk about our intentions?" Willow asks, waving her yellow journal. "Because let me tell you, I have some doozies."

We laugh as Mom answers, "Definitely."

RIGGS

T HE SKINNY CHORUS kid in me may hate pep rallies, but the high school principal in me straight-up loves them.

I've spent the past hour trying to talk Mr. Dander into letting the drum line go full out and do a whole routine for the pep rallies, and the man is blocking me at every turn. I'm beginning to think he's got a personal vendetta against showmanship.

"The marching band has a tradition to uphold," Mr. Dander sniffs.

"Tradition of boring," I mutter, reaching the heavy plastic banner as far as I can safely go on the twenty-foot ladder.

"To the right a little," Mr. Dander says.

"No, he just needs to lift it some," Mrs. Hayes cuts in. "Put your glasses on."

"They are on!"

The ladder wiggles beneath me and I hold steady. "I'm trying to reach a nail that's permanently lodged in here," I call down. "So I don't care if it's sideways, it's going on that nail and that's that."

Mr. Dander and Mrs. Hayes both mumble something I can't hear, and probably don't want to. I have no idea how I got roped into doing this, but next time, the senior boys' basketball team seems like the perfect group of candidates to get this up.

"How old is this thing?" I ask.

"It's a perfectly fine banner," Mr. Dander huffs.

"The wolf looks like a second grader got hold of some design software in the early two-thousands," Coach declares as he wanders into the gym. "I've been trying to get Mrs. Hayes to approve a new one for years."

"Unnecessary expense," Mr. Dander says.

"Oh, like new plumes for the marching band hats is a legitimate expense?" Coach shoots back.

Sweat beads on my forehead as I try once more to reach the nail that's taunting me, mere inches from me in the painted white cinderblock. "Are you sure this is the right spot?"

"Maybe come down and move the ladder," Coach suggests.

"Almost…there!" I finally manage to hook the banner onto the nail.

Coach claps his hands once. "That's it. I'm ordering a new one. Mrs. Hayes, you better approve it. It's not nearly as much as those stupid plumes."

"The plumes aren't stupid!" Mr. Dander insists, his voice as reedy as an oboe.

I shift my body to tell them both to stop acting like children, but the ladder wobbles again. Only this time, there's no getting my balance back. Panicked, I grab for anything to hold on to, and my hand finds the edge of the banner.

Except my hands are sweaty, and my fingers don't find purchase on the plastic.

"Finlay?" Coach sounds concerned, and he should be, because the banner and I are going down.

Fuck.

IT SHOULD SHOCK no one when I say that high school kids are easily distracted. And that's especially true when the ambulance arrives at school, siren blaring, causing every kid with a view out the front windows to completely dispatch with their studies and focus instead on the fun that is watching their idiot principal get loaded onto a stretcher.

Magnolia had gotten to my side in the gym almost immediately, despite having a class to teach. Worry pinched her brow as she scanned me, bruised head to questionable ankle.

"Damnedest thing," Coach told her. "He was hanging a banner one second, then he'd fallen the next."

I didn't bother mentioning that nothing would have happened if he and Dander hadn't been arguing like preschoolers. Or that I probably shouldn't have been so high up on the ladder without someone at the bottom to steady me. Or that maybe I should have just moved the stupid ladder in the first place.

Either way, off to the emergency room I go, in a ridiculous ambulance because Mrs. Hayes insisted on calling it.

Magnolia holds my hand as the paramedics prepare to load me into the back, letting go only when one of them looks at her and says, "Ma'am?"

She releases me with no small amount of reluctance, and it makes my heart fucking *leap* at the care in her eyes. "I'll meet you there," she promises, leaning to maintain eye contact even as the paramedics shut the doors.

She's already waiting for me when we get there, because apparently she beat the ambulance. It makes sense, as the driver took his sweet time, but I still smile at my love when we arrive. Even though everything hurts and I'm tired.

"Don't you dare go to sleep on me, Riggs," Magnolia snaps.

"So bossy," I croak. I make myself stay awake, because it's almost certain I have a concussion. I got one during my stint in the Marines, and it's a feeling you don't forget.

The paramedics hand me off to the waiting ER staff, and I don't know if Magnolia got there early enough to clear the way for her to accompany me, or if she's simply that intimidating to the guys wheeling me into the back, but either way, she stays right by my side.

It takes a while, but eventually the diagnoses come: mild concussion and a broken ankle. I'm grateful that it's my left one, but it still isn't the best news.

The doctor looks between both of us after the cast is put on. "I'd like you to stay overnight for observation," she concludes.

"What if I watch him?" Magnolia asks.

The doctor hesitates.

"Please?" Magnolia continues. "I can promise you I'll keep just as good an eye on him as anyone here."

After another moment, the doctor nods. "Okay. You bring him back immediately if he shows any signs of something being wrong."

I breathe a sigh of relief. I was not looking forward to an overnight stay, and I have to wonder if Magnolia sensed that. It's not that I have anything against hospitals, but I'd prefer not to be here if I don't have to be.

It's another hour before I'm discharged and hobbling into the passenger seat of Magnolia's little car. It was no small feat for her to shove the scooter they insist I have to use into the back seat, and now, she flops with a huff into the driver's seat.

I suppress a grin as I look at how adorably disheveled she is. "I'm sorry."

She frowns. "You have nothing to be sorry for. This is my fault, Riggs. I—god, I'm so sorry."

"This isn't your fault." I hurry to reassure her, waving my hand up and down myself. "I did this all on my own."

She pulls out of the parking lot and shakes her head firmly. "This has *everything* to do with the curse. It might be worse now that I have the veilstone."

I look over, surprised that she'd think the stone would have anything to do with my falling. "Magnolia, seriously. I fell because I was clumsy. That's it." Then I peer at the speedometer and look in the side mirror to see a line of cars behind us. "Um, Mags?"

She tightens her hands on the wheel in what is certainly a ten-two death grip. "Yes?"

"I think you need to speed up."

"I have to be careful with you, Riggs."

"Okay, but you need to drive faster than twenty miles per hour. It might honestly be *more* dangerous to drive this slowly."

"I know what I'm doing," she states flatly.

"If you mean you know how to piss off an entire line of cars that stretches who knows how far back, then yes, you're doing great." When she doesn't respond, I try another tactic. "I really just want to get home, Mags. Can you please speed up?"

She sighs. "I hate it when you say please."

I laugh. "Why's that?"

"Because then I almost *have* to do it. It's annoying." She speeds up to thirty-five. It's still below the speed limit, but it's better than nothing.

She looks over at me when she finally pulls into her house's driveway. "We're staying at your house. I've got to get some things first."

I opt to stay in the car, and she's back quickly. It's another five excruciating minutes before we're finally at my house, and five more before I've made it to the couch.

I wince as I stretch my leg out while Magnolia hovers beside me, biting her lip.

"You're home now, so you can be honest. How bad is it?"

I'm about to answer *everything hurts and I'd really like to take a nap* when my front door bursts open. I startle, knocking my ankle against a pillow and nearly howling in pain. "What the fuck?" I growl.

Magnolia whips around. "Aspen?"

Aspen doesn't bother with niceties. "I brought tea."

I raise my eyebrows. "Please come in."

"Let's not beat around the bush. You're in pain, and instead of immediately getting to business and brewing something up that will actually take away that pain, my sister over-corrected. She drove too slowly, she stopped at our house instead of bringing you immediately home, and now she's standing there like a lump on a log instead of helping me make you feel better." She pauses. "Am I right?"

I grimace. "Yes."

Magnolia lets out a squeak of protest. "I was *about* to—"

Aspen sweeps out of the room and aims straight for the kitchen. Judging by the racket she's making, she's not wasting any time.

Magnolia exhales, and her shoulders slump. She turns those caramel eyes on me, and they're full of sorrow. "I can tell you're in a lot of pain," she mumbles. "Your aura is sad."

I chuckle and pat the couch. "Sit with me."

She lowers herself gingerly, perching on the edge and

going to an absurd amount of trouble to not touch me. "I've messed everything up."

I reach for her hand, and she looks at it.

"Come on, my little witch," I cajole softly, wiggling my fingers. "Don't bail on me now."

She huffs a watery laugh and finally takes my hand. That familiar spark pushes into me, and I smile. "Better?" she asks.

"Much," I say, then raise our hands so I can kiss hers. After a moment, I start to feel better. "Are you doing that?"

She ducks her head. "It's the least I can do."

I smile. "Not that I don't appreciate the good vibes—I do —but I've had a broken leg before. This is nothing."

"I mean about this." She gestures around with her free hand. "Us."

I squeeze her hand. "We'll be okay. This is a speed bump. A little bumpy bump."

"This is more than a *bumpy* bump, Riggs. It's like we're at the beginning of one of those 'Final Destination' movies, where stuff will keep happening to you until…" She stops, swallowing and shaking her head. "No. I won't even think that, let alone say it."

"This isn't part of the curse."

"It probably is," Aspen says as she breezes back into the room.

I growl again. "Not helpful."

She shrugs, utterly unapologetic. "I know this 'dating a witch' thing is new to you, so let me be super clear: if Magnolia says that what's happening is part of the curse, then guess what?" She blinks at me. "This is where you answer my question, Riggs."

"I thought it was rhetorical." Magnolia's helpful touch notwithstanding, I'm still a little snappy thanks to the pain

I'm in. "I'm guessing you want me to say that if Magnolia says that it's part of the curse, then I should believe her."

Aspen raises a thin eyebrow, and the small gesture tells me exactly what she thinks of me right now.

I sigh. "In case you haven't noticed, I've had a shit day and my entire body hurts."

Magnolia squeezes my hand. "Apology accepted."

Aspen sniffs. "We'll see." She shoves a mug in my face. "Drink this. All of it. It doesn't taste great, but there's nothing to be done about it. It's effective, and you won't care when you're on cloud nine in five minutes."

"Hang on." Magnolia plucks it out of Aspen's hand before I can grab it.

Aspen rolls her eyes. "I love a good trick as much as the next sister, Mags, but now is not the time. He really needs to rest. And before you say anything, I dialed the intensity back since he has a concussion."

Magnolia smells the tea anyway. Apparently satisfied, she hands it over.

It smells earthy, like mushrooms and moss. I take a tentative sip, then suppress a retch. "Oh god."

Magnolia chuckles as Aspen crosses her arms. "Faster you drink it, faster it's over."

It tastes like what I imagine one of those poisonous caterpillars would taste like. Which is to say: disgusting. I toast the two of them, mutter a half-hearted "Bottom's up," and chug it as fast as I can.

"Attaboy," Aspen praises, a rare smile crossing her face.

Magnolia takes the mug from me as I attempt to not hurl, because, my god. "That…was not okay," I manage to get out.

"I'll go get you some water." Magnolia rises and lets go of my hand.

As soon as she's out of the room, Aspen pins me with a glare. "Listen to me, and listen to me well."

I blink a little slowly, already feeling the effects of whatever she put in the tea. "Mmkay."

Aspen steps closer and drops her voice low. "Magnolia is a fucking treasure of a woman, but she's even more of a powerful witch coming into her own. You will do as she asks, you will believe every fucking word that comes out of her mouth, and you will. Not. Fuck. This. Up. Do you understand?"

I think I might be drooling. I wipe at my chin and miss. "Dafugdidyouputanherrr?"

She smirks. "Do you understand?"

"Yep. Nofugup." I try to give her a thumbs up. Am I floating?

"Aspen!" comes Magnolia's exasperated voice. "Seriously? What did you do?"

"Nothing you can't handle, little sis," Aspen says.

My world goes dark.

Magnolia

"WE HAVE TO go to karaoke." Riggs already sounds out of breath from getting dressed. He got crutches and a walking cast yesterday, but the stubborn man still refuses to take any more help than is strictly necessary. Which means everything takes him double the amount of time it normally does.

"I'll be fine," I insist, pulling on one of my flowery skirts and chemistry joke T-shirts as we get ready for school. I've spent the past week at his house, and curse or not, it hasn't escaped notice that I've been here ever since I had that one random thought about wanting to wake up here more. I glare up at nothing. *Universe, if you could please* not *attempt to make my every random thought come to fruition, that'd be good. Some of my thoughts don't need your attention. Probably most of them. Cool? Thanks.*

Riggs bends down to put on a shoe from where he sits on the bed. His shoulder muscles ripple beneath the fitted button-down and the dress slacks he insists on wearing hug his thighs. I bite my lip at the memories of last night, when I was the one hugging his thighs as I edged him mercilessly, knowing he couldn't move as easily as normal and taking full advantage.

"What's got you grinning like that?"

I snap back to attention. "Nothing."

He snorts. "Doubtful." He stands from the bed and hobbles until he's behind me, slipping his hands beneath my shirt and kissing my neck as he runs his thumbs along the underside of my breasts. "Looked like you were thinking of something naughty."

I shiver. "Maybe."

Licking at the sensitive skin just below my ear and then kissing it, he murmurs, "I would love nothing more than to pull you onto that bed and make you sit on my face until you came." He cups my breasts and squeezes. "Feeling the way your thighs shake as you come, listening to your moans of pleasure."

A deep ache settles between my thighs as my nipples harden. He turns me around, kissing me deeply and grabbing my ass so hard I hope it leaves a bruise. I reach down for his belt, and he groans, stopping me. "We have to go," he mutters, a dose of reality punching through the lust.

"Do we have to?" I palm his dick, and it thickens beneath the pants.

"Fuck," he groans again, then attempts to pull himself away from me. "We really do. High school waits for no one."

I drive us again, much to his displeasure, but at least it's thirty-nine miles per hour. Which is faster than yesterday, and that's all he's getting.

As we pull into the lot, he looks over at me. "We're going to karaoke."

"I told you, I'll be fine."

"I don't want you *fine*. I want you better than fine. You're wearing yourself down to the bone, and it's just over a week before your Gathering."

He's right, and I sigh in defeat. "Okay."

He smiles happily, and after I put the car in park, he leans over for a kiss. "Aspen would be so proud of me."

I laugh. "You're scared of her, aren't you?"

He pulls a face. "You didn't see the way she got all growly and mean after she drugged me. You'd be scared, too. I swear to you, Magnolia, I half expected her to extract a blood oath from me."

"Well, the tea was basically the same thing," I shrug.

He pales.

I laugh. "I'm *kidding*." Sort of, but he doesn't need to know that. She really did a number on him. I read her the riot act about it once he passed out, and Aspen was unrepentant. Swore it was to ensure all went well at the Gathering, and the way she said it, how deadly serious she was, I let it go. The only good part was that the intention she brewed into it was only to ensure his safety, and nothing else. No messing with feelings or actions.

Riggs eyeballs me. "You're not funny. Quinton wasn't kidding—your sisters are a menace."

"Maybe." I fight a smile.

He opens the car door. "Let's go torture some high school kids, shall we?"

We separate at the top of the steps, and Ava finds me in my classroom before the first bell. "You know the secret's out, right?"

I squint at her. "Which secret? Because it feels like I have a lot of those at the moment."

She purses her lips. "You know what? Fair. I mean the you-and-Riggs-are-an-item secret. Whole school knows. Kids are buzzing." She jazz-hands the last word and grins.

"Eh," I say, straightening papers on my desk.

"Eh?" she repeats. "*Eh*? Is that all you're giving me? Woman, this is the juiciest thing that has happened in this school since Mr. Dander and Coach got into a yelling match over whose turn it was to get the profits from the concession stand."

"That *was* fun," I recall. "Wonder if we can rile those two up again…"

"Focus, woman. Besides, you can top it if you and Finlay ramp things up," Ava says, leaning in and whispering. "Hold hands…maybe kiss?"

I raise an eyebrow at her. "School just got started. Are you that bored already?"

She lifts a shoulder. "Eh."

I swat at her. "I see how you are, mocking me. You're the worst."

The warning bell rings and she starts to retreat, her smile wide and deep red lipstick fresh. "You know I'm right."

"Doesn't mean I'm going to do it," I shoot back.

"Riggs and Mags…sitting in a tree…" she singsongs.

I jerk my hand along my throat and hiss, "Stop it! I don't need the drama and the students don't need the distraction."

She cackles as she leaves the doorway.

Shaking my head, I turn my attention to the tenth graders filing in for homeroom and get myself ready for the day. Happily, I've figured a way to keep my emotions in check while I teach, and mainly that's simply a matter of refusing to think about the sex god that is Riggs Finlay.

Well, that and a safety pin that I keep in my skirt pocket. Turns out the tiny prick of pain it delivers is just enough to keep me from wandering off-track. And we're not going to talk about how many pin pricks I have in my fingers. What's important is that I no longer have a bunch of horny teenagers in my midst.

Well, no hornier than usual.

A MERE TEN pin pricks and eight grueling hours later, Riggs and I are on the way to karaoke. Or at least, we would be if he would hand over the keys he somehow swiped from my tote when I wasn't looking. "Riggs. Give them to me."

He holds them up in the air, well aware that my short self has no hope of getting them. "I can drive, Magnolia. I'm *begging* you to let me. For one thing, I'm tired of riding shotgun, and for another, I might honestly lose my shit if I have to go under the speed limit anymore. Just because you have silver in your hair doesn't mean you need to drive like a granny."

I gasp. "You did *not* just call me a granny, old man."

He chuckles. "Then quit driving like one. Now come on." He opens the passenger door and gestures for me to get in. "Let me drive. We've wasted enough time, and I know you want to change."

With a huff, I climb in. "I'm not happy about this, you know."

He winks and leans down to place a kiss on my cheek. "I know. But you love me."

I roll my eyes. "Not really sure about that right now."

As he starts the engine and begins the hour-long drive to Al's, I breathe. Because breathing is all I can do. Despite joking around with him, I'm terrified something will happen: a distracted driver, a blown tire that causes us to lose control, an eighteen-wheeler loaded with logs that all come loose and fly toward our car...these are the things that go through my head.

Breathe.

After a tense scrying session with Mom and Willow last night, in which we tried and utterly failed to see what Kera has been up to—which I'm positive was my fault since I've never been able to scry—Mom grabbed my hands in both of hers. When I finally met her gaze, she said, "You can't control everything, Magnolia. We're witches. Our control only extends so far. What you *can* do is control your reactions."

I'd rolled my eyes, because it was a trite metaphorical pat on the head and she knew it. Then she'd jerked my hands toward her, and I swear I felt her palms heat up. It got my attention.

"It was a mistake to let you wander this long," she said, "focused only on the life directly in your face and ignoring the Universe, but what's done is done. You need to learn to control your *reactions* to things, Magnolia. Your emotional reaction. Your cognitive reaction. Your physical reaction. Your spiritual reaction. They all work together. Master your reactions, and your magic will intensify."

I mulled her words over on the walk to Riggs's house afterward, and they came back to me now. What she spoke of, the mastery of my reactions, isn't something I can simply decide on and it will happen. I need to be thoughtful about it. Methodical. But I only have a week before the Gathering, and the more we all work toward figuring out how to lift the curse, the more I understand just how powerful it is, and the amount of energy that it will take to break it.

And in the meantime, I have this beautiful, wonderful man beside me. A man who loves me. *Me*, the woman who still won't sing for her family. The woman who still can't bring herself to change the way she dresses for school even though the clothes are beginning to feel like a skin that needs to be shed. The woman who still goes by Seven at Al's.

I'm so tired of being scared. And I'm so *pissed* at Kera for her stupid jealousy. I want to bring the world down on her, to cause her decades of pain and fear the way she did to me. Because what was the point of it all? I can't believe that she wielded such a strong curse simply out of jealousy. There had to be another reason. Was our family a threat? Was it just me? Fucking Kera. And her mother, Ginger. Because how could Ginger have allowed something like this to happen, let alone continue? She had to know. Kera could not have done something that powerful so young.

"Mags?"

I look over at Riggs. "Hmm?"

He quirks a smile at me. "You're doing it again."

Only then do I realize that the entire car is vibrating, and not simply because Riggs is driving too fast. "Oh." I shake the emotion off, and immediately the vibrations cease.

"What's going on in that beautiful head of yours?" He sends a pointed glance to where my hand clenches the center console.

I force myself to relax, easing my fingers off the hard plastic and leather one at a time. I guess I need to work on my unconscious reactions, as well.

He reaches over and lays his palm, heavy and grounding, on my thigh. I lace my fingers through his and inhale. Hold. Exhale. Close my eyes and do it again. Inhale. Hold. Exhale.

"Magnolia?" he prompts.

I reach for my makeup bag and grab a navy pencil to line my eyes. I pull the visor down, studying myself in the rectangle of light. *Who are you?*

You know who you are, the voice says.

I'm not so sure.

Yes, you are.

Well, maybe I am, but that doesn't mean it's any less terrifying. Trying to reconcile Seven with chemistry and

Magnolia with karaoke, for one thing. And then there's the witch part. It grows with every passing day, where I wake up and find some new, previously unrealized power is within me. How am I supposed to make sense of all of this *and* break a curse in a week?

Finally, I answer. And since he asked a direct question, the answer is one hundred percent truthful. "I don't know if I'm prepared to be who I am, Riggs."

He squeezes my leg, and after a moment, he says, "I do."

I choke out a noise that's half-sob and half-laugh, then look over at him. "Yeah? Wish you'd let me in on the secret."

Outside, the sun sets to our left, bathing his profile in a golden haze. I will myself to remember this exact moment: the confident set of his jaw, the outline of his muscular arms in the maroon Henley he's wearing, his full, kissable lips. He glances at me, his gaze lingering a little longer than I'd prefer given that he's driving, then turns into the parking lot. Once he parks, he kills the ignition and angles his body to me. He holds his hands out for mine, and when I clasp them, the comforting rush of power moves between us.

The sun's rays are still behind him, like his own solar-made aura, as he looks at me. "You are so strong, Magnolia. And brave, facing this curse head-on the way you are."

I want to wave him off, but he tightens his grip. Beaten, I mumble, "I don't really have a choice *but* to face it."

His voice is gruff when he speaks. "Yes, you do. You're making choices every day, whether you see them or not. You're Magnolia Rowan *and* you're Seven. You're fiercely protective of your family, and you're a champion for your students. You're incredibly sexy. You have a voice fit for the angels *and* devils, and you're ridiculously smart. But it's your heart that I know best."

I swallow, barely able to take a breath.

Riggs simply smiles. "Your pure, effortlessly beautiful heart. I've already felt the way you've changed me, Magnolia, and it's like nothing I've ever felt. So yeah, I think you are absolutely capable of becoming who you're meant to be. Because you're *already* her. You are a treasure. A wonder. An absolute force of a woman. And it is my undying honor to be yours."

I can't speak as he raises my hands to his mouth and kisses my knuckles. His gaze travels over my face, and lingers on my lips before finally settling on my eyes. With a gentle smile, he lets go of a hand to push my hair behind my ear, sending a knot of emotion into my throat.

I blink quickly to keep the tears at bay. "You really think that?" I manage in a hoarse whisper.

He nods. "With all my heart. Magnolia, Seven, witch, chemistry teacher, sister, bed hog. I love every part of you."

I choke out a laugh. "I do not hog the bed."

He shakes his head sadly, placing a hand over his heart. "Oh, my love, you most definitely do. I have the bruises to prove it."

"Whatever," I mutter, but I do it with a smile.

He laughs, then tips my chin up with his fingers. "You ready to sing, Seven?"

"Yeah," I rasp. I clear my throat and speak clearly. "Yes. Let's do it."

We make our way a little slower than usual to the door, thanks to his crutches and the gravel of the parking lot. I wave to Carol once we're inside, then take care of putting our names on the list while Riggs gets us drinks.

"How many songs you two singing tonight?" Carol asks, holding an unlit cigarette in her hand.

"Bad day?" I nod at the cigarette.

"Bad week," she answers, then forces a smile. "Nothing for you to worry about."

The words sting, and I know it's because we've never shared anything personal. I look at her, *really* look, and she looks much more frail than normal. And I can't take it. I can't take being scared and worried and never letting people know the real me. *All* of me. So after I write our songs down and toss a couple of twenties in the jar, I hold my hands out.

"Can I help?"

She looks at my palms like I have snakes in them, then flicks her gaze up to me, suspicious. "What are you doing?"

I shrug. "Something I should have done years ago. I'll start with this: my name isn't really Seven. It's Magnolia. Magnolia Rowan. I live in Sacred River, and I'm a chemistry teacher at the high school there."

Carol blinks twice. "Okay," her voice raspy as always. "You a serial killer?"

"Um, no?"

"Plan on confessing any sins?" she continues.

One side of my mouth hitches up. "Definitely not."

"Then seriously, Seven, what are you doing?" Her aura is dim and is the palest I've ever seen it. Normally a bright yellow, this evening it's a soft white, as though the yellow is too tired to appear.

"Helping you," I reply. "If you'll let me." Even though I'm pretty sure I could have made her feel better already, I don't want to do anything without her permission. It feels wrong otherwise.

She rolls her eyes, clearly over me and this conversation. "Sure, whatever your name is. Tree?"

I laugh. "Magnolia."

She puts her hands in mine. "Well, let's get this moving, Magnolia. Two minutes and it's karaoke time—and you know we start right on the dot."

So I try. I close my eyes and pull the Universe's attention to me, and ask it to bring its healing powers to Carol. To make her feel better and to help those around her as well. To give her a sense of well-being, and contentment, and to smooth out any complications in her life. If she has family, I want them to be close and happy, to connect and remember how much they love each other. And above all, I want Carol to find peace and happiness and love for herself, no matter what that looks like.

Squeezing her hands one last time, I open my eyes and peer at her. "You feel any better?"

She frees herself from my grip and gives me another once-over. "No, but honey? It's awfully nice of you to try."

I study her, attempting to catalog whether she looks any different than before, but there's nothing. Her aura remains unchanged. Everything about her remains the same.

Maybe I did it wrong. Or maybe I'm not as powerful as I think I am.

"Pretty sure Riggs is waiting on you." She gestures to where he sits. "Y'all want to go first tonight?"

I shake my head. "Somewhere near the beginning is fine." I turn away, then swing back when Carol calls my name.

She grins ruefully. "Seriously. Thank you. I don't think it worked, but whatever you did, I appreciate it."

When I join Riggs at the bar, he pulls me to him in a tight hug, and I turn so that I'm tucked between his legs as he sits on the stool.

"Everything okay?" he murmurs in my ear.

I shrug. "Yeah. I think I was being silly." It's hard to shake the disappointed failure, and it's far too similar to the way I felt growing up for comfort.

Carol kicks the evening off with a soaring rendition of Adele's "Rolling In the Deep" before calling the first person up. I lose myself in the songs and the feel of Riggs's comforting arms, and after half an hour, Riggs goes up.

"This one's for Seven." Riggs gives me a salacious wink as

something starts up that I don't quite recognize. It's a laid-back, groovy track, and I finally realize what it is when he starts singing. It's Drake's "Hold On, We're Going Home," and my stupid heart swells as he sings.

Riggs pulls off some serious moves up there, sliding across the stage despite his cast, like he might have practiced in his room a lot more as a kid than he'd be willing to admit, and straight-up croons to me, singing how he knows exactly who I could be. The lyrics are deceptively simple, but they're powerful, and perfect for this exact moment. He pulls the crowd in to help him on the chorus and gestures for me to join him on stage.

Obviously, I get up there, smiling and laughing as he turns to me and gives me everything he's got, hamming it up for me and the crowd. They love it, and so do I. And when the song is done and he hobbles off the riser, suddenly half-lame again like he didn't just Smooth Criminal all over the damn place, it's my turn.

"This one's a little on the nose," I admit to the crowd. "Sing with me anyway."

Kylie Minogue's "Can't Get You Out of My Head" begins to play, and the whole place sings the la-la-la part with me as I shed everything out of me except the song. No worries about the curse, no sadness about not being able to help Carol, no terror about Riggs or anyone in my family getting hurt. Just me, my voice, and the music. The relief is palpable and cool as the bass thumps in my chest and I sway my hips back and forth, channeling Kylie and singing about being unable to get a certain boy out of my head. My eyes are closed for the first verse, and as we all launch into the chorus, I open my eyes.

It's stunning.

The entire place is lit up with happy auras. Pinks and purples and oranges and yellows, sparks of glitter shooting into the air with giggles and bad falsettos as we sing the song, and it's the best feeling in the whole world. To know that I'm the one doing it, pushing my delight into everyone, and getting it right back...it's amazing. I could do this forever.

Which is why it's a real drag when I black out.

Magnolia

I COME TO consciousness slowly. Voices murmur in hushed, worried tones. My sisters. My mother. Riggs.

What happened? I can't remember anything, and it's too much effort to open my eyes just yet. Judging by the smells and sounds, I'm on the couch at home. I take deep breaths, trying to rally myself. A shadow blocks what little light I sense from behind my eyelids, and a warm palm comes to rest on my forehead, the weight of it grounding and comforting as always. *Riggs.*

"I think she's coming around."

"Dim the lights," comes Willow's voice.

Someone snaps their fingers and near-darkness seems to descend.

"Show off," I croak as I manage to open my eyes.

Aspen scoffs, and her worry is a palpable taste in my mouth. "Shut up," she chides softly, kneeling in front of me. "How are you?"

I try to sit up, and a wave of nausea rolls over me. "Not good," I answer, cradling my stomach. "What happened?"

"We were kind of hoping you could tell us," Clementine prods, standing between Juniper and Jasmine.

"Give her some water." Mom steps forward and hands the glass to Aspen, who holds it while Riggs helps me rise up on my elbows. I extend my hand for the glass, but I'm so shaky that Aspen helps me bring it to my lips. When I'm finished, I lay back with a sigh.

"I can feel all of you staring at me." I close my eyes again.

"They're worried." Riggs's cedar scent envelops me as he sits on the couch and guides my head onto his lap. "Can you tell us what you remember?"

I search my memories. "I was singing on stage," I begin slowly, "and I was having the best time. Everyone's auras were…ecstatic. I'd never felt so happy just from singing."

"Aw," Juniper coos. "Isn't it amazing?"

"Could you not make this about you?" Jasmine snarks.

Even though my eyes are closed, I know the twins are making faces and gesturing at each other, and the utter normalcy of it is comforting. "Yes, seeing them is amazing," I manage, my voice still not quite normal.

"More water," Mom urges. "Riggs."

An amused, quiet huff comes out of him as I feel him reach for the water. "Want some?" he murmurs.

Opening my eyes, I let him help me with another sip, then prop myself back up on my elbows to drink more. The effort is more than it should be, but I fight through it. "Anyway, I was singing, felt amazing, saw the auras, then…nothing."

"Did you do anything before that?" Aspen asks. "Anything that would have triggered it?"

I consider. "I tried to help Carol."

Mom and Willow look at each other, but it's Aspen who asks, "Who's Carol?"

"The woman who runs karaoke night," Riggs answers.

I meet his eyes. "I told her my real name and said I was a

I yank on another patch of deadnettles. "Which knock-off?"

"The one that puts you out like a light," she grins like a fiend.

I laugh. "We're a little notorious for our teas, Clem. Don't you think they're going to check before just drinking whatever we give them?"

She raises a perfect dark eyebrow as she snips off a cluster of black locust from the pioneer tree, then inhales the aroma from its white petals. "Our bees love these flowers. Best honey in the world."

It takes a minute, but I finally get where she's going. "Wait. We're spiking the *honey*." Wonder laces my words.

"Bingo. Kera is the only one who insists on using honey in her tea, so we'll make sure to have plenty of it available."

"I've been helping Mom and Aspen with spell research as well. We're getting there."

"It's why Mom's got all of us out here at the crack of dawn."

"That and she's just evil," I joke.

"Accurate."

When we all arrive back at the kitchen with baskets of flowering plants, herbs, berries, mushrooms, and a few river rocks and some mud for good measure, Mom looks everything over. "This will do it," she announces.

Quinton and Riggs high-five each other. "Told you we got the right stuff," Quinton says, a satisfied smirk on his face.

Clementine snuggles into him. "You did great, babe." She meets my eye and giggles.

Riggs watches it all, his keen eyes catching everything like always. When he swings his questioning gaze to me and I give a minuscule nod of confirmation, he laughs silently. We all disperse a few minutes later, and Riggs pulls me back outside and studies me, tucking a piece of hair behind my ear.

"How are you feeling?" His voice is low and charged, and it is unbearably sexy. I didn't know how much I'd enjoy having someone be so concerned about me.

"You mean other than the fact that we're all preparing to wield some wild witchy magic in a week in an effort to break a curse we only just realized I've been living under for more than two decades?" I joke.

The lines crinkle around his blue eyes as he smiles down at me. "Other than that."

"Better than the other night."

"Good. Because I've been terrible."

Immediately, I tense. "What? Why?"

"Easy, tiger," he chuckles, running his hands up and down my arms. "I didn't mean to get you riled up. It's just..." He looks around. "I've missed you in my bed," he murmurs, leaning into me and nuzzling my neck, his strong hands coming to rest on my waist and pulling me close.

"Riggs," I whisper, all thoughts of curses and spells falling out of my head.

He continues. "Turns out I really like having you in it. And I had a *lot* of ideas of things to do on a lazy Saturday morning. None of which I got to do this morning." He pulls back and looks at me, his blue eyes darkening with desire. "So I think we should go to my place."

"You do?" I ask, my voice a little breathless.

"I do," he answers, his voice deep and reverberating through my chest.

For a moment, I think that maybe Clementine slipped something into our water, because my heart has sped up and my breaths are coming faster and faster. But that's not it. No —it's simply that Riggs is in front of me, telling me he wants me, and I want him in return. It's as simple and complex as that.

Because I get it now. Love, *this* kind of love in particular, is more powerful than any magic. It is the kind of love that leaves me breathless with desire, and wonder, and an unwavering willingness to do whatever it takes to keep him safe.

So I let him take my hand and walk us the short distance to his house, his cadence a steady *step-thump, step-thump* in his walking boot. And when we get inside, he turns me against the door, threading his fingers through my hair and exposing my neck to his lips. He kisses me, nipping that sensitive spot right where shoulder and neck curve into each other, and I shiver with need.

"Your skin tastes like sunshine," Riggs says, tightening his grip on my hair in one hand while the other traces a line down the side of my breast and waist before sliding into the elastic of my panties. "And now I want to know what the rest of you will taste like."

Without hesitation, he drops to his knees on the hardwood floor, the hard plastic of his boot scraping across it as he pulls my loose, long skirt up and over his head and yanks my panties down and off. In an instant, his tongue is on me, licking up the seam of me before homing in on the tight bundle of nerves and swirling.

"So good," I gasp, then let out a moan at the glorious sensation, my hips beginning to rock of their own accord. "My god, your mouth feels so good." I close my eyes and lose myself to it, letting nothing invade my senses but pleasure. Pure, undiluted pleasure. Riggs groans against my core, and the sound sends me soaring.

My legs begin to shake, and he takes one and tosses it over his shoulder, shifting his weight so he's propping me up against the door and keeping me steady, all while his tongue, hot and wet and slick, glides over my center. In no time at all I'm right on the edge, and he teases me with his finger, pushing it into me, but only a little. "Riggs," I moan through gritted teeth. "I need more. Give me more."

He doesn't. I swivel my hips, one hand on the doorknob and the other gripping his shoulder through the cotton of my skirt, chasing the orgasm that he's keeping just out of my reach. The bastard.

He chuckles, and I must have called him that out loud, because he says, "Call me whatever you want, sunshine, but you're not coming until I say so." Then he stops, pulling away and standing, my skirt falling away as he does. A pulsing yellow aura surrounds him, deep and golden like the rays of the sun he called me, and I fist his shirt to yank his mouth to mine.

The kiss isn't gentle. It's teeth and lips and tongue, and I taste myself on him as I jump into his arms, the move as thrilling as it was the first time. He grips my ass and takes us to the bedroom while I swivel my hips against him, grinding against the hard plane of his abdomen, the need for release no less intense than it was a moment ago. When he loosens his hold on me and my feet hit the floor, we waste no time in getting our clothes off, and then it's me who's shoving him onto the bed and then his back, crawling up his body until my knees bracket his head.

With my hands on the headboard, I meet his stare, the aching need for release almost unbearable. "Make me come, Riggs," I demand. "Now."

His eyes flash with heat as his arms wrap around my thighs. "Fuck, Magnolia," he growls. "You're sexy as hell when you tell me what to do, you know that?"

I lower myself to his mouth, and he takes me. My eyes close and my head tips back in relief as a moan escapes. He sucks my clit, and the pleasure is so intense I nearly jerk away from him. Then he pushes his tongue into me, fucking me with it, before swirling back to press hard against the spot just below that bundle of nerves, and I'm bucking against him, fucking his face as my hips move on pure instinct, my blood fizzing with intensity, until finally, *finally*, I come.

"Fuck!" The word is almost a scream as the orgasm crests, my entire body convulsing with the waves of pleasure coursing through me.

Without warning, Riggs pushes my hips up and scoots out from under me. "Don't move," he growls, moving onto his knees behind me. My core is still pulsing when he pushes into me from behind, filling and stretching me so completely that the orgasm kicks right back up. My inner walls squeeze him, and he curses. "I'm not going to last if you keep doing that, Magnolia," he warns, seated deep within me.

"I don't care," I gasp, bucking my hips against him, desperate and needy for more. "Please, Riggs, fuck me."

He pulls out almost to the tip, then slams home again. "Like that?" he asks, his voice low and raspy. Sexy. He does it again, pulling out slowly, then ramming into me.

"Yes," I rasp. "God, yes. Please. More." I tilt my head to the side, exposing my neck. He bites down on it, still pulling out slowly and thrusting into me hard, one hand finding my breast and pinching the nipple as the other holds onto my hip, his fingers digging into my skin. "Yes," I hiss, then beg again. "Please."

"How bad do you want it?" His fingers find my clit again, swirling around it.

I arch my back, holding onto the headboard. "So fucking bad, Riggs."

"Fuck, baby," he grunts. "Don't move."

My knuckles go white from the effort. "I need you to fuck me so hard, *please* Riggs."

Finally, he snaps. Then he's pounding into me, his hips pistoning into me again and again, and I sigh in relief. Because when we're like this, two people making each other feel good, interested in and wanting only the other's pleasure, that's when I can relax and just *be*.

His fingers dig into my hips, his short nails surely leaving half-moon indents in the skin, and the painful pleasure of it is perfect. And still he thrusts, unrelenting, as another orgasm builds, driving toward release with every motion Riggs makes behind me.

"I'm almost there," I pant.

"Let go of the headboard." He slides a hand along my back to guide my head to the mattress, and the shift in angle is miraculous.

I groan in appreciation. "Fuck, Riggs, your cock." My voice is deep and breathy. "So good. So fucking good. Oh god —" I can't speak anymore, because his fingers are pressing against my clit, circling, and it's as good as a detonation. I begin to soar, and Riggs goes with me, pumping once, twice, before cursing and stilling, his cock twitching inside me as he finds his own release.

I breathe hard, gulping in air as my upper body collapses, spent, onto the mattress. Behind me, Riggs bends to my back, peppering it with gentle kisses as he pulls out of me. "Lay down, sunshine. I'll bring you a washcloth."

He's off the bed and running hot water in the bathroom in an instant, and I take the opportunity to see what damage we've wrought this time. I've gotten better at containing my reactions here, too, but there comes a point where I simply... *can't*, and that's when I'm coming. Honestly, who can blame me?

As Riggs walk-thumps back into the room with his cast, he catalogs with me: the salt lamp is tilted on its side, because that poor lamp is always affected, and the closet door is open. "Not bad by you," he says, a satisfied smile on his face.

I hum as he tends to me, the washcloth the perfect

temperature, his touch gentle. When he's done, he angles his body to the hamper and balls up the washcloth, tossing it like he's going for a three-pointer. Then he lays back down, gathering me into his arms.

I snuggle in, my head on his chest, and breathe in his cedar scent. He kisses the top of my head and threads his fingers through my hair. I trace his muscles, appreciating the compact solidity of them that comes only with age, the fine dusting of hair that's more silver than black.

When Riggs speaks, his voice is gravelly. "I want this all the time, Magnolia."

I tip my head back to meet his eyes, the irises a warm turquoise in the light. Even though I think I know what he means, I joke, "What, orgasms?"

"You, Magnolia." He doesn't take the bait. "I want you. I love you, and I want *you*, all the time, with me. Waking up with you is a dream come true. Seeing your beautiful smile first thing in the morning, tumbling into bed with you at the end of the day. Being able to touch you, hold you, kiss you." Then he cups my face and bends down, pressing the gentlest of kisses to my lips. "Stay with me."

"Stay the night?" I whisper, hardly daring to believe what he's really asking.

"Stay always," he answers, sending my heart into overdrive. "Live with me. Be with me. I know your family is important to you, and I don't want to get in the way of that. You have utterly and completely changed me, my little witch."

All I manage is a squeak. Inside, I'm a puddle of gooey emotions.

His eyes, so calm and serene, the complete opposite of how I'm feeling in the face of this, search mine. "You don't have to answer now, and even if it's yes, you don't have to move in immediately. I will always want you, and I will wait as long as you need. I. Am. Yours." He peppers my face with kisses with that last part.

It takes everything I have not to cry. Because getting to this point, lying in bed with a man who knows all the parts of me and still loves me, even the parts that scare me and may always keep him in danger, is almost too much. "How?" I croak. "How are you so perfect?"

He huffs a gentle laugh. "I'm far from perfect, my love."

I shake my head. "No. You are. You are completely and totally perfect, and you make me want to cry and also put you in bubble wrap."

He raises a dubious brow. "Um...thanks?"

I sniff and give him a watery smile. "What if this doesn't work?"

"You mean next week?"

I nod.

He takes a deep breath, holds, and releases it, making my head rise and fall. "Then you'll try again."

It sounds so simple. *Try again.* Is that even possible? When was the last time I saw any group of witches try to take down another witch's curse? Right: never.

"I don't know if I've done enough. Haven't studied enough. Read enough texts. Gathered enough herbs and plants and freaking river mud, of all things." I wipe at a rogue tear. "And if it's not enough? If it fails? What if something happens to you, Riggs? I couldn't—" I choke on a sob.

"Hey, hey," he says softly, wrapping his arms even tighter around me. "It's going to be okay."

"You don't know that. You can't possibly know."

"Okay, you're right, I don't know. We've been over this, remember? You have to let me do things my way. You can't control Kera right now, and you can't control the world around us."

He sounds like my mother. "I control my own emotions

and reactions—believe me, I know. But if that's not enough…"

He flips us over and settles between my legs, the hard plastic of his boot scraping gently against my skin. Grinning mischievously, he takes a nipple between his teeth. "Then we'll figure it out. But right now?" He closes his mouth over the tight bud, then licks and sucks until I'm a squirming mess beneath him, all thoughts of the curse gone.

Later, when I wake in the middle of the night, I'm wrapped tightly in Riggs's arms, my butt to his crotch, only the flat sheet on top of us. The salt lamp, put back to rights, glows dimly in the dark. Could I do this? Stay here? Let myself love and be loved like this? I want to. God, I want to so badly.

A sense of determination sweeps over me. I'm going to fix this. I have to. Because losing Riggs is not an option.

MAGNOLIA

THE MORNING OF the Gathering arrives muted and cool, the grass shiny with dew, the river covered with a low mist that spreads over the muddy banks. It's the first day of autumn. Behind me is the bed that no longer feels like mine, and in it sleeps the love of my life. There was no question that I needed to wake up here, to be with my family as the clock rolled over into the day that would change everything. And even though I haven't given him an answer on living with him, I've also stayed with him every night since.

It's a teacher work day, and last night, Riggs didn't hesitate to come with me. Just grabbed a gym bag and tossed everything he needed in there after we returned from karaoke, then walked with me through his backyard and onto our property. And when we'd all looked at him last night as we stood around a literal miniature cauldron bubbling on the porch with one of the more innocuous brews we planned for our guests, he'd caught on and skedaddled up to stay in my room the rest of the evening. It was well past midnight when I finally came to bed, and he

A shadow crosses her face. "Definitely not. She was Persephone's friend."

Ah. Aunt Persephone is Mom's sister, and definitely the one to take the most risks. I'd wager that Persephone is why Mom has always tried to limit her magic to our land, and flat out wouldn't allow us to use it off the property growing up. Not that there was much to do before we were sixteen, and not that I, in particular, did much of anything, anyway. "Is everyone awake?"

Mom hums in confirmation, then tilts her face to the dawn, eyes closed. "Persephone, Calliope, Chloe, Phoebe, Iris, and Dahlia will be here soon."

The rest of Mom's sisters. They'll stay with us, and most will sleep in Mom's room, because the room will simply grow to accommodate them like it did when they were growing up, thanks to a spell Mom's grandmother put on the house. Come to think of it, I wonder if that's what started the house's journey toward sentience. Or whatever its deal is. Anyway, Jasmine and Juniper will bunk together like they did when they were kids, and Willow and Aspen will join them. Hazel's room will go to Kera and her mother, and I'll keep my room since we really have no clue how tonight is going to go.

Sometimes other families join us, and since they're not related, the house doesn't accommodate them. I'm pretty sure the house hates anyone who isn't family. Though, come to think of it, it's been pretty nice to Quinton, and even Riggs.

I file that nugget away to address later.

Right now, it's time to begin the day.

THE HOUSE IS LITERALLY a glitter fest after my aunts arrive. I don't know if it's simply been tense with everything going on with Kera's curse—totally a possibility—or if it's just feeding off my aunts' infectious energy. Either way, puffs of gold glitter float from nowhere as though the house is absolutely beside itself with glee. And I get it: the aunts are a walking personification of wacky quirky witches, complete with patchwork skirts and jackets, boots that look like they're better suited for the 1800s than the 2020s, and hair that could use a good brushing and some serious products.

I love them.

We spend an hour getting them settled, the atmosphere thick with happiness as they flit about, reacquainting themselves with the house and shouting to each other from room to room. You'd never know they were just here last year with the way they're acting.

Calliope sniffs the air in my room and raises a red brow at me. "Really?"

My cheeks burn, then I remind myself that today, of all days, I need to be strong. Brave. To literally speak up for myself. So I straighten and throw my shoulders back, then answer decisively. "Yes, really. Just because you and the rest of the aunts don't seem to believe in love, it doesn't mean I don't."

Calliope's eyes widen in surprise before crinkling into a smile. The house sends what I assume is an approving puff of glitter into the air. "Magnolia, that's wonderful." She opens her arms wide for a hug. I step into her ample embrace, knowing it's unwise to refuse. She'll simply make me come to her, and I learned as a child it was better to not be physically dragged by invisible hands into Calliope's arms.

"It is?" My voice is muffled with how hard she's smooshed me against her chest, and some kind of crocheted lace tickles my nose.

She grabs my upper arms and holds me in front of her, looking me up and down. "It is. I must say, getting dicked down suits you."

I choke in surprise, my eyes immediately watering as I whack my chest. "Oh my god," I sputter. Calliope is easily seventy-five. I think I'm scandalized.

She rolls her eyes. "Please, Magnolia. We're both adults. If we can't talk about a good dicking at this point, then when can we?"

I'm dying. Absolutely dying. I keep coughing, my face probably red as a beet, as I try to pull myself together.

She sighs and twirls her hand, producing a bottle of water that she waves at me.

I unscrew the lid and take a sip, and in a few moments, I'm able to take a full breath. "Wow, Aunt Calliope. That was…unexpected."

"Pfft. Now tell me all about him," she commands, threading her arm through mine and leading me back downstairs. "Then we'll talk about that veilstone you've got in your pocket."

My lips quirk up. I'd not told the aunts about the veilstone yet, but if anyone was going to sense it, it was going to be Calliope. "I knew you were my favorite aunt for a reason."

An hour later, after telling all of Mom's sisters about the veilstone, Riggs and Quinton return to the kitchen. They come to a comically screeching halt as every woman turns to them, and for a moment I half expect to hear the sound of a Western movie standoff float into the air.

Riggs is the first to speak, and honestly, I couldn't be more proud of him. "Afternoon, ladies."

Quinton jumps in. "You must be the aunts."

Mom takes them through the introductions, and I catch Riggs glancing at me. He raises his brows in a silent *how are you doing* query, and I dip my chin back. *I'm good.* His lips tip up, then he turns back to meet Calliope, getting pulled into one of her infamous hugs. Whatever she says makes him blush, and I'm glad to know I'm not the only one getting scandalized.

Not two minutes later, Aspen appears by my side. "She's here."

RIGGS

I CAN TELL by the way Magnolia stiffens that Kera must have arrived. There's a domino effect, too, where each sister picks up on her energy and seems to still, followed by their mother Daphne and all her sisters. Within moments, the kitchen has gone quiet. Even the house seems to be holding its breath.

And can we talk about the house for a second? What the *hell* is going on? The damn thing is shooting glitter out of light fixtures, and I'm almost positive that the kitchen door was locked to me and Quinton for a second. I'd tried to get us in, and I'd swear the door was stuck. Then Quinton tried, and it opened without a problem. "Perks of being part of the family," he'd said and winked at me.

I'm not proud of the jealousy that shot through me when he said that, seeing as how it was over Quinton's relationship with a *house*.

Daphne paints a too-broad smile on her face as she excuses herself to get the door, and the kitchen springs to life again. I make a beeline for Magnolia, only to be blocked out by the rest of her sisters. Glancing back at Quinton, he gives a subtle shake of his head and I get it. This is a sister thing. A witch thing. Neither of which I am. With a resigned sigh, I follow Quinton onto the back porch.

"How much do you know about what's going to go down today?" he asks as the door snicks shut behind us.

I rub at my jaw. "I'm still getting used to this witch stuff, so," I shrug.

He looks at me thoughtfully. "It bothers you? The not knowing?"

Well, shit. Am I that transparent?

Quinton chuckles. "Don't worry, man, I get it. My introduction to this family was trial by fire, you know that. First it was the Elysian Blossom, then her damn sisters drugged me —*twice*—but none of it mattered. Because I loved her from the minute I saw her. She drove me fucking crazy, but I had to be hers. There was never a choice."

I study him, and finally ask the question I've tried not to think about. The last fission of doubt. "Did you ever believe it was the magic?"

"Nah." His reply is instant. "Clementine did. Hell, sometimes she *still* thinks it was the love potion that brought us together. And in a sense, it was, only not the way she believes. My family's dynasty was riding on getting the Elysian Blossom's essence back into production for our perfume. I came down here for that purpose and that purpose only. What I didn't anticipate was being thrown on my ass by a pixie-sized botanist with a huge chip on her shoulder and an attitude as big as Texas."

I shove my hands in my pockets. It's inspiring, the love he has for his wife, the utter devotion. Dude is straight-up besotted.

"You don't think what you and Magnolia have is only due to magic, right?" His question isn't surprising.

I blow out a breath and recall everything that's happened

up till now. The immediate attraction I had to her when she was merely Seven to me. The way I looked forward to seeing her every week, and how I was mesmerized by the way she seemed to transform when she got on the tiny stage. The reaction my body had to simply *touching* her. How, after we began seeing each other, she started to unfurl and bloom like the very flower she's named after. How I did the same, only I didn't realize it at the time. The love in her eyes when it's just the two of us. The way I can make her come undone, and the way she does it to me. "No," I finally answer. "It's not the magic. It's real."

"Glad you admitted it. It's nice to have another guy around here."

I tilt my head at the kitchen. "So about today."

"Listen." Quinton steps around to look me dead in the eye. "I know you're a lot older than me—"

"Fuck off."

"*And* trust me when I say that today is not about us. Our job is to stay as far out of the way as they want us to be, and to come only when called like good little boys."

"Clementine's got you tied up good, doesn't she?" I quip.

"I mean, yeah," he laughs. "But I'm willing. And it might be hard, standing by and letting Magnolia do whatever it is that she needs to do today, but you have to."

The air chills as two women emerge from the kitchen. I don't recognize them, but know instinctively it's Kera and her mother. Quinton shifts so that he's not an inch from me, and when he gently knocks into me I realize it's because I am literally growling. I clear my throat.

Kera looks me up and down, her eyes a cold gray, her hair raven black and cropped short. Her cheekbones are high, angling down to an almost viciously pointed chin. Her lips are a glossy red, and they part now in a thin, calculating smile. "Riggs Finlay, right?"

Her words send cold dread skating down my spine. How does she know who I am? I shake it off. In this day and age, it's not hard to figure out who someone is, even though Magnolia and I don't use social media. I keep my hands in my pockets and nod at her. "Right." I deliberately don't say it's nice to meet her. It isn't.

The other woman is an older version of her daughter in almost every way, except her hair is a thinning pale red shot through with white. She puts out even less of a welcoming air than Kera. "I'm Ginger. This is Kera. We're cousins of the Rowans. And you are?" She aims the question at Quinton.

"Clementine's husband, Quinton," comes the answer.

Ginger says something else and Quinton answers, and all the while Kera stares at me. As her eyes travel the length of my body, lingering on the walking boot before making their way back up to hold my gaze, I finally understand. The feeling of unease, of someone poking around in my head, is visceral, as though slime is seeping through my veins and slowing me down.

I blink to break eye contact, fighting back a wave of nausea as another instinct tells me to visualize a blanket drifting over my thoughts. I grunt, my body tense with the effort, and surprise flits across Kera's features before her eyes narrow.

It's all the confirmation I need, and I see red. It's been her this whole fucking time.

Magnolia

RIGGS.

  I look around and realize that Kera and Ginger have gone outside without me even realizing it. Two thoughts go through my head simultaneously: one, she's a lot stronger than I realized if she managed to divert my attention from her, and two, she's too close to Riggs.

My body flushes with heat and I'm in front of the door, ready to throw a punch into Kera's smug face, when Aspen appears beside me.

"Wait."

"Why?" I growl, glaring outside. "I'm going to kill her."

Aspen's hands curl over my fists and her voice is low. "Not yet. Besides, murder isn't a good look."

"I think now is a perfect time, actually."

Willow's voice rises behind me. "Let's give our cousins some tea."

Breathing unsteadily, I let Aspen move me away from the door while Willow prepares to step outside. The honey that Kera insists on using in her tea is infused with the herbs that create our Truth Tea blend, and they're completely untraceable. We're starting there.

In the sudden quiet of the kitchen, the aunts all cast curious glances at the three of us. Persephone speaks up. "What are you doing?"

Mom locks eyes with me, and I know it's my story to tell. But why will they believe me, especially Persephone? She's the one who was—*is*—friends with Ginger, after all. I swallow the lump of shame in my throat and shake my head. "Discussing tea."

"My dear, I say this with all the love in my heart: that's bullshit. Your aura screams you're lying," Phoebe says, her dark bun precariously balanced on top of her head. She nudges Calliope beside her. "Surely she knows we can see that?"

Startled, I glance at Juniper, who grimaces in confirmation. Crap. How did I not think about the aunts and all their various gifts? Of course some of them could see auras. Behind me, Riggs's voice sharpens and everything in me screams to get outside.

So I do. The aunts can wait.

Outside, Kera smirks at Riggs, who glares back at her with so much hate that it's a wonder Kera's even standing. A quick glance at Riggs tells me something's happened, but that he's fine. A spike of anger blasts through me, and the skin beneath my skirt pocket heats. The veilstone. It's reacting to my emotions, which isn't surprising. Its bond with me has only intensified, and while I'm still learning what it does, I knew today was the day to have it with me at all times. I can only hope that Ginger and Kera don't sense it the same way that Calliope did.

"Tea?" Willow asks innocently, holding the tray with practiced ease. "The two of you came outside so quickly that I didn't get a chance to offer."

The women accept the cups, and Aspen pours the tea. Passing a look between them, Ginger and Kera smell the tea, and Ginger sips it.

"Honey?" Willow smiles at Kera. "I remember you prefer yours a little sweet."

With a saccharine smile at Willow, Kera dips the spoon in the honey, then swirls it into her tea. She takes a tentative sip, then a larger one.

Perfect.

Quinton steps forward. "Got some for me?"

It takes everything in me not to blanch. I have no idea if Quinton takes honey in his tea, and if he does, things will get interesting.

"Me, too." Riggs steps forward, and I'm pretty sure he growls at Kera.

Riggs, who definitely takes honey in his tea.

Riggs, who doesn't know the full plan, because he didn't need to.

Riggs, who, like Quinton, is highly sensitive to our magic.

Willow glances at me, and all I can do is widen my eyes in an *I have no idea what to do* expression.

We can't manage any kind of swap, because Willow brought out enough for everyone. All I can do is watch help-lessly as Riggs dunks a healthy amount of honey in his tea. Quinton does, too.

Shit.

Aspen turns her caramel eyes to me and narrows them, but what am I supposed to do? Knock the tea out of both men's hands?

I love them, but these two men are being such...*men* right now that I'm momentarily overcome by exasperation.

Seriously. Men.

Anyway.

"How've you been, Kera?" I ask as Willow excuses herself

to take the tray back inside with a mouthed *I'm so sorry* in my direction.

She shrugs. "Busy," she says airily. "You?"

"Same."

"Looking forward to tonight," she continues.

"Same." Can I help it if my voice is flat and full of repressed rage? No. No, I cannot.

"You seem...tense." Kera finishes off her tea.

"Oh, you know," I reply. *Just preparing to undo this curse you landed on me for no good reason and trying to keep you out of my head and keep everyone around me safe, no big deal.*

The door bursts open behind us and everyone streams out, breaking the growing tension.

"Clementine!" Quinton enthuses, opening his arms wide. "My darling Clementine," he croons as she steps into his arms. He hugs her tight and starts humming the old song, which I'm frankly surprised the Canadian knows.

Clementine chuckles. "Hey, hot chocolate. I need your help. Come with me." She takes his hand and begins leading him in the direction of their house, situated on the back right of the property.

I catch on quickly. We need these two out of here. With a barely-repressed glare at Kera, I step forward and grab Riggs's hand. "Oh, that's right. We need you two to finish up with the tents."

"But we finished," Riggs says, utterly oblivious to what's happened to him, bless his heart.

I drag him off the porch. "There's one more."

"There is?"

Mom draws everyone else's attention away from us, and I increase our pace.

"You're going too fast," Riggs complains, his boot scraping through the grass with every other step he takes.

"Clementine!" I hiss. She slows and we catch up.

As we slow to a regular pace, Quinton looks at his wife, then me, then Riggs. "Fuck me," he breathes. "We're dosed, aren't we?"

"Is that what's happening?" Riggs asks.

I push happy thoughts into my touch, and instantly, Riggs's face blisses out. "Yep," I admit. "Just truth tea, but with all the energy of the equinox today, plus a full moon, plus all the witches around...you two didn't have a chance."

Riggs waves an arm in the air. "Don't care. You're making me so happy right now, even though I hate that woman back there, and her mom, too—they are *not nice*." He pouts that last part like a put-upon toddler.

Clementine snickers and angles Quinton's hand toward my free one. "Do it to Quinton."

"Hell no," Quinton says, yanking his hand out of my reach. "Damn witches."

"You'll feel soooo nice." Riggs almost slurs the words.

Quinton looks at him and flattens his lips. "Brother, you are a mess."

We get the men into Clementine and Quinton's house and sit them both on the couch. My sister looks over at me. "What kind of sports are on right now?"

I shrug. "Football? Maybe? I don't know."

"Just give me the remote." Quinton holds his hand out. When Riggs tosses it to him, Quinton turns on the television and looks back at us. "It was the honey, wasn't it?"

"Daaaaamn." Riggs draws out the word and slumps further down into the couch.

"It'll only last a couple of hours," Clementine assures them. "I have no idea how long the bliss that Riggs is feeling will go for."

"She tried something on me," Riggs says. "Felt slimy."

I go rigid. "She *what*?"

"I shut her out, though, because I'm awesome." He gives

me two thumbs up, and it eases the frost building inside me. "Maybe I *do* have some of my great-grandmother's magic. Wait. Grandmother's? Great-grandmother's. I dunno," he shrugs happily.

I look at Clementine, then Quinton. "I swear I didn't know my touch would do all…" I wave my hand up and down Riggs's slumped form, "…*that.*"

"Just stay here, Q, and keep that one in check." Clementine points at Riggs.

Quinton wraps his wife in his arms. "Okay. I love you. I'm worried about you, but I know you'll take care of yourself and our girls. Because I want boys, but no way are they boys, because I just don't think that's a thing, and I'm babbling, and whatever, damn truth tea. Be careful, sprite."

Clementine melts into him, and the two of them look at each other so gooey-eyed that it's kind of disgusting. I glance at Riggs.

"Hugs?" he asks, holding his arms out from where he's pooled into the couch. His aura is a ball of sunshine, and the love beaming out from him warms me from my toes to my hair follicles.

Laughing, I lean down, and he yanks me on top of him into a crushing hug. When he finally eases up, I rise onto my elbows and meet his gaze.

His eyes, those beautiful bright blues, come into focus. "I love you so much, Magnolia."

I smile gently. "I love you, too, Riggs."

He runs a finger from the top of my forehead, down over my nose and lips, and then pulls me to him for a soft kiss. "I believe in you." His voice is low. "You've worked so hard. You're so strong, and wonderful, and I don't deserve you, but I'm selfish enough that I'm keeping you anyway. And I will love you even if she turns you into a troll."

I snort. "Thanks, babe."

"You're welcome," he says seriously. "I'll be cheering you on from where I'm apparently becoming one with this couch."

I bite my lip to keep from laughing, and he releases me so I can get up.

Quinton shakes his head. "Fucking *witches*, man."

Magnolia

B
Y THE TIME we return to the main house, everyone has scattered to prepare for the evening's festivities. Clementine retreats to the silence of her greenhouse, and I follow, content to put my chemist skills to use with her as she works on a new blend of scents for her and Quinton's first perfume together.

My emotions are all over the place. One minute I'm breathing easily, ready to take Kera on and undo decades' worth of damage. The next minute, I'm a jittery mess, worried about what I'll learn. It's terrifying and exhilarating, and I want to face her *and* run away all at the same time.

The veilstone, on the other hand, pulses calmly and steadily in my pocket, not worried at all. I suspect it understands how important this evening will be, and when I wrap my palm around it, it pulses even harder. Happy.

"You gonna marry the veilstone instead of Riggs?" Clementine gives me a teasing shove as we stand at the counter running along the inside of the greenhouse. "You touch it enough."

My cheeks heat. "It's weird, but I swear it's in a good mood."

"May I?" She holds her hand out, then gasps in surprise when I drop it into her palm. "It's warm. It's *pulsing*." Wonder laces her words.

"It's been doing that all day. I think it knows how important today is. What I'm going to need it to do."

Clementine holds the stone up to the light, turning it this way and that, studying it. Its normally milky-white color is a bit more translucent than normal, making the fissure I caused upon receiving it much more noticeable. "Does it always change like this?"

I shake my head. "Just today."

"Equinox thing?" she guesses, handing it back to me.

"Maybe," I shrug, conducting my own inspection before tucking it back into my pocket. "Or maybe a Rowan witch thing."

"Or maybe a *Magnolia* Rowan witch thing. Even though we're not witches," she adds.

"You know, at this point it's just embarrassing the way you deny it, right?" I tease.

She pretends to be insulted. "I think the term is derivative. We're so much *more* than mere witches. We're guardians. Guides. Interpreters. Givers. Creators. We're the physical manifestation of nature's incredible gifts, and if more people would just open themselves up to the possibility of wonder, then I think they'd be able to bring some magic into their own lives."

I gape at her. "Clementine, that's…beautiful."

She stares at me. "No shit."

I bark out a laugh. "Well, if you come up with a better term than 'witch,' let me know. Until then, I'm wearing my title proudly."

The veilstone pulses against my hip, and I realize what a

shift this is for me. I've never been *proud* of being a witch. I've simply been one. Even with Ava, my best friend growing up and still today, I've never talked a lot about being one. How... strange. Why have I been like that? Why haven't I acknowledged such a fundamental part of myself all these years? Because what Clementine says is true: we are so much more than our title, and I've been almost willfully blind to it my entire life. Never truly embracing who I am and what my gifts could really be until recently.

Until Riggs.

"Where'd you go?" Clementine asks, snapping me out of my thoughts.

I smile at her. "Just...thinking."

I'M BY MYSELF, almost at the willow tree, when Kera calls my name from behind me. Exactly as my sisters and I planned. My heartbeat is steady, the veilstone pulsing in my skirt pocket as I turn. "Kera."

Her gray eyes flash and her small ruby mouth pinches as she demands, "What did you put in the tea?"

I don't hesitate. "That's not how this is going to go, Kera. What did *you* do to *me* at our Gathering all those years ago?"

She jerks her head back, then chuckles as understanding seems to dawn. "Oh, I see. So *that's* what's been going on. I've been wondering why it's so different, watching you now."

I go still. "What do you mean, watching me now? You've watched me before?" I step toward her, the anger building sharp and quick inside me. "Do you have any idea how creepy that is, not to mention invasive and rude? What is wrong with you?"

She rolls her eyes. "Magnolia. Get over yourself, will you? You're standing there acting like I'm the big bad wolf when you're the one who made it so bad."

"What are you talking about?" I demand. Aspen and the rest of my sisters have appeared, fanning around us into a circle along with my aunts and mom. Ginger is also here, though I can sense her unease.

"Wow." Kera's voice is thick with sarcasm. "This feels far more serious than it needs to be."

"You cursed me!" I yell, completely done pretending and ready to throttle her within an inch of her life. "Of course it's serious. *Decades*, Kera. You've had me messed up for decades. Why?"

"Truth tea," she states flatly, ignoring the question. "You gave me truth tea when I got here."

I step toward her, but Willow grabs me and cuts in. "It was the honey. Not the tea."

Kera waves an accusing hand at us, her black hair skimming her cheeks. "See, that's the problem. You and your high-minded sisters are absolutely convinced you're better than us. Always. Sharing secrets and potions and knowledge among yourselves, while the rest of us are on the sidelines, grasping at the scraps the Rowans deign to throw out. Do you have any idea what it's like to be on the outside of your family, Magnolia?"

"Yes!" I seethe. "I absolutely do because *that's what you made happen.*"

She shakes her head. "I didn't do that. *You* did that to yourself. Honestly, Magnolia, do you really think I could be so powerful at sixteen as to wield some kind of curse that lasts for, what did you say, decades? Give me a break." She turns in a slow circle, eyeing everyone around us. When she faces me again, she pins me with a glare. "I would have given anything to have been a part of this. Instead, all you did was push me away, year after year, not even bothering to let me into your circle. Do you have any idea how painful that was? How unnecessarily cruel?"

I flinch, my fingers curling around the veilstone in my pocket. "What are you talking about?"

Her laugh is cold, harsh. "Of course you didn't notice. You never did. How much I wanted to be a part of your family, and none of you would have it. I was number eight, you said, and that was the worst number of all. Not your precious seven. But look around: where's your seventh? *Gone*. I wanted to be a part of it, Magnolia." She points at her chest. "Me. And you couldn't be bothered."

Above us, the sky bends toward dusk. The actual witching hour. This is when we're supposed to counteract the curse. The thing is, I'm beginning to suspect that the only curse I have to counteract is mine.

Her eyes flit to my pocket. "When did you get the veilstone?"

I stiffen. Of course she knows. "It was a gift."

She rolls her eyes. "I know it was a gift. You may have spent your entire life running from what you were meant to be, but *I* haven't. Not that you'd know that, because…" She gestures around the circle, as if that explains everything. "I bet you don't even know half of what that stone can do for you. You know why? Because it's been the one thing the Rowans haven't had. Guess who has one? Us. Mom and me. Just our small little clan of two, but we have one." She reaches into her pocket.

"Stop!" Aspen surges into the circle, holding her hands up as if to defend me against whatever Kera is about to throw.

Kera sighs. "Honestly, Aspen. This isn't some showdown between wizards with their wands like in a fantasy novel,"

cled by two sets of seven, and as I turn to look at each witch, meeting their eyes and searching their auras, I know, without equivocation, that each of their intentions is good. Even Kera's. Even her mother's. Because while Kera may not be sorry for what happened, she also has no ill will.

The words come as if they've lain dormant for hundreds of years instead of mere decades, and my throat opens wide to let them out. It doesn't matter who is around. Nothing matters except stepping into myself.

"Universe, and all that makes you what you are: the nature surrounding us, the wind on our faces, the water slaking our thirst, the fire in our hearths, the earth providing everything we could ever need: I come before you with an apology in my heart. I am sorry. I have not acknowledged you and your power. Instead, I have been quiet my entire life. I have only observed, and compared myself with those whom I watched. I have never fully embraced what we are—what *I* am —choosing to see only the barest of magic and using even less."

The veilstone heats up to an almost uncomfortable temperature, but I hold on, letting its vibrations seep into me. The wind rises around us, bringing the heady, lush scent of magnolia flowers with it.

Looking up at the moon that's beginning to rise over the willow tree, I continue. "I have been wrong, and I have wronged you in return. Please forgive me. And with that forgiveness, I call on you to remove this curse that I have put upon myself. Allow me to sing once again without fear. Allow me to step fully into the power I have shunned. I want to be better. Allow me to become who, and what, I am destined to be."

A crack of lightning strikes, sending the scent of ions to mix with the magnolias. Chemistry and nature, fused into one. I open my eyes, not sure when they closed, and see that each circle of witches is surrounded by a bright white light, as though their individual auras combined to form a cohesive circle of beautiful magic. The veilstone's vibrations reach a fevered pitch, forcing me to release it or risk getting burned, and as I remove my hands, it hovers in the air, then rises. The circles of white arc toward it, meeting it and forming a dome of rainbow-infused light above us.

My chest thrums, then waves of nausea grip me. I don't know if I lose my footing, but suddenly I'm weightless, surrounded by my sisters and Kera, all of them supporting me as thick, shiny tendrils of black smoke emerge from within me, curling out and slithering, one after the other, up toward the dome of light.

I watch, horrified, as the tendrils continue to pour from my chest, and Aspen curses softly behind me.

Wind whips around us, blocking out all sound except for the frenzied beating of my heart. I'm frozen, unable to move for what feels like an eternity, and finally the curls of darkness leave me. I shift my gaze, watching as they hit the dome. The rainbow hues darken as the light absorbs the smoke, turning gray, then black, before it turns in on itself, pulling all the light from the circles into a tight ball of black, then exploding. Streaks of white burst above us like fireworks, and another bolt of lightning breaks across the sky. The veilstone drops to the grass at my feet.

The silence that follows is deafening. Dazed, and a little woozy, I manage to lean down and pick up the veilstone, noting its coolness as I squeeze it and put it back in my pocket. I breathe and take stock of myself. I feel...lighter. Whole. A low energy flows through me, the power I've tamped down for too long now simmering just below the surface.

"Did it work?" Jasmine's voice is soft, and I realize that everyone—my sisters, my mother, my aunts, Kera, and her mother—is bunched around me, no longer in circles, but simply surrounding me.

My throat works on a swallow. I did it. *We* did it. It takes a moment, but I finally speak. "Yes. Yes, it did," I confirm, a smile spreading across my face.

Mom grabs me into a hug, and Aspen's arms join hers. In moments, I'm at the center of a family sandwich, and the happiness, the lightness, I feel is almost too much. Like I'll float away if they let go.

"I've missed you," Aspen whispers. "So much."

"I've missed you, too."

"All I ever wanted was to be included," Kera sobs. "This hug is amazing. Is this what you all are like all the time?"

We all laugh as we break apart, and Kera's expression stills. "Oh, *dammit*," she says. "This truth tea is still working, isn't it?"

RIGGS

"THE MARCHING BAND has never sounded better." Mrs. Hayes is in the announcer's booth with me, and she gives me a knowing look as they march off the field.

I arch a brow. "Remarkable, isn't it?"

"Really is," Ava chimes in.

Together, we all turn to Magnolia, whose eyes widen. "What? I thought they needed a...boost." Her cheeks get pink, and she's so damn adorable I can hardly stand it.

"Get over here, my little witch." I pull her to me and relish the feel of her snuggled into my arms.

Ava sighs happily as she watches us. "I love this so much. You two are disgusting, and I love it."

Mr. Taylor, who it turns out is the voice of the Sacred High Wolves and not only the school janitor and faculty party bartender, clears his throat. "Look. I appreciate all of your company, but could you leave? The second half is about to start, and I can't be distracted."

Ava glances longingly at the opposing team's defensive coordinator, a hulking mass of a man who takes up a lot of space in this booth, and who I've gathered is her boyfriend. "But Mr. Taylor—"

"Nope," he cuts her off.

"Okay, everyone, let's go." I herd us all out and down into the stands, where the students are way more into the game than I would have figured they would be. We're a month into the season, and we've lost as many as we've won, but they're just as riled up as if it were the first game.

Calls of *Hi, Principal Finlay* and *Hi, Miss Rowan* follow us as we descend the concrete steps, followed by the inevitable whispers from the girls about the fact that I'm holding Magnolia's hand. Apparently, it's "romantic" and "swoonworthy." All I know is I'm grateful she's finally letting us be out in the open.

Hell, she put *everything* into the open after the Gathering. Her transformation has been beautiful to watch this past month, from subtle things like incorporating her Seven wardrobe into her everyday wear—she says she feels more in control when she wears her Docs to teach in—to the more obvious like singing along to songs without worry, and using her magic at school. It's nothing too startling, even though I knew she was hesitant at first. Once she saw that the students thought it was "bad-ass," though, she was all in. It's helpful that she's learned to control her emotions so that they don't affect those around her; I was getting tired of breaking up all the make-out sessions that were happening around the school.

Although I have to admit, it was nice to know that those kids were doing it because Magnolia was thinking about me.

I've rewarded her in my office accordingly. Multiple times. Because Magnolia's also got a way to make it where no one can see or hear us when we're, shall we say, *occupied*.

In fact…

I nod at Ava and Mrs. Hayes, then tug Magnolia in the opposite direction.

"Riggs, what are you doing?" she asks.

I don't answer as I tighten my grip on her hand and lead us around the stands. As she giggles behind me, I make a note to thank Mr. Taylor for ensuring I got a copy of all the grounds keys. In moments, we're at the door leading beneath the bleachers.

Magnolia's face is the picture of innocence as she asks, "Principal Finlay, where are you taking me?"

I grin and unlock the door. "Ever been in here?"

She shakes her head and follows me in. It's a small room piled with tables, chairs, various types of sports equipment, and lawn care stuff. It doesn't smell great, but I don't give a shit.

Wordlessly, I close the door, and darkness falls around us. I pull her to me, claiming the gasp of surprise on her lips. Her green apple scent surrounds me as I thread my fingers into her hair and tug lightly, angling her mouth where I want it. She moans, and the sound goes straight to my dick. Almost immediately, the temperature in the room rises.

"Easy, tiger," I chuckle against her lips. Because while she *can* control her emotions and how they affect the surrounding environment, she doesn't always.

"There's an easy fix for that, you know." She shucks my jacket off, and hers hits the floor with a soft *thwack* a second later. Her hands go to my belt, but I swat them away and push her against a table. A soft whine escapes, but she stops as soon as I begin to undo her pants and kneel before her. Which is a hell of a lot easier now that the walking boot is gone. "Riggs," she breathes.

I make quick work of her, getting a boot off and yanking her jeans and panties down, then pulling them off one side. An aching sense of need—*her* need—pulses through me, and the shock of it is almost enough to knock me on my ass. "Fuck," I bite out, trying to get my breath.

"Now," she demands. "Your mouth. My pussy."

"I'm tr—"

Her palm is on the back of my head, slamming my face against her, before I can finish. Not that I'm complaining. My dick presses painfully against my jeans as I grip her ass and suck her clit into my mouth. Her answering moan is all I need to know I'm where she wants me. That, and the fact that she's not letting up on my head.

"Eat me like I'm the last fucking thing you'll ever have," she growls.

Seriously. This woman is going to make me have a heart attack with how fucking sexy her commanding me is. How much it turns me on. So I obey. Fuck yes, I obey. I feast, tossing her bare leg over my shoulder for better access as I plunge my tongue into her. Her hips writhe as she moans above me, and I give her exactly what she wants. Licking, sucking, swirling, tasting. Wringing every whimper and moan out of her like it's my goddamn job.

"So good, Riggs. So fucking good. Just like that," she praises, riding my face as she seeks her pleasure. Above us, the crowd cheers, and all I can think is, *damn straight*.

Right when she's on the edge, her legs shaking around my ears, I pull away. "Need to be inside you," I whisper hoarsely. "I have to feel you come around my cock. Please."

She groans in assent as she pulls me up by my shirt, yanking my lips to hers and opening immediately for me, tasting herself on my tongue. A pulse of heat blasts against me.

Chuckling, I undo my jeans. "You like that, don't you?"

"I like it all, Riggs," she answers. "Now shut up and fuck me."

I push into her without preamble, and we both groan

loudly. She's so fucking perfect. I pull out and thrust in again, and again. My little witch doesn't want soft and sweet right now. Another blast of heat hits me, and sweat runs down my forehead.

Magnolia curses and yanks my shirt off. "Skin. Need your skin." Then she groans as I hike her leg up and push her ass onto the table. Her nails rake across my chest and I hiss at the delicious pain. She follows it up with pinching my nipples, and pleasure streaks through me. "More, Riggs. More."

I go faster. Harder. Things are definitely falling around us in this room, but I'm lost to the feel of her exquisite pussy enveloping me, tightening more and more as I fuck her. "Magnolia," I grit.

"I need—" she starts.

"I know." I pull her up, still joined, and walk us to a wall. When I thrust again, she moans.

"Fuck yes," she gasps. "Ohmygod ohmygod omygod."

I nearly black out at the pleasure. It's almost too much. My legs are screaming, and I've lost all sense of time and space. It's animalistic. Feral. Hungry. I can't get enough.

"I'm gonna—"

"*Now*, Mags."

She yells as she comes, her pussy squeezing me so hard I see stars. I follow with a shout, the both of us clinging to each other as we ride out the most intense orgasm of my life.

The crowd yells above us and Mr. Taylor's voice rings out. "Touchdown, Wolves!"

Epilogue

M Y HANDS ARE a little sweaty as I write my song selection down. As I hand the pen to Riggs, Carol looks at what I wrote and grins at me. "Excellent choice." She looks so much better than a month ago, but hasn't been inclined to tell me if I had anything to do with it. Honestly, I don't think I did.

Riggs chuckles as he reads what I wrote. "How am I supposed to top that?"

I shrug and smile happily, even though I can't seem to stop shaking. Riggs finishes up, then walks back to join our group. I grab the pen once more and write down a second song. "Can I do these back-to-back? Ignore Riggs's request."

Carol's grin gets even bigger. "Who'd you bring with you?"

"My family."

My *family*. All of them. And I am so nervous that I'm an absolute mess. I turn to join them back at the bar, my stomach flipping at the sight of them.

Mom. Jasmine and Juniper. Willow. Aspen. Clementine and Quinton. Even Hazel is here, looking so sleek and out of place next to the rest of us as she smiles brightly at my grimace. And there, off to the side and beaming, is Riggs.

Love of my life.

No—more than that. He *brought* me to life. And as he holds his arms out for me to step into, I'm so grateful for him. "Thank you," I whisper.

"For what? Being awesome?" he jokes.

Hazel slides a glass of soda over the bar to me. "Can't believe we get to hear you sing after all these years!"

I look at the soda, then at the bartender's questioning glance. He takes it without a word and replaces it with a tumbler of whiskey.

Hazel eyes me. "Um, who are you and what did you do to my sister?"

I laugh. "Believe it or not, Zelly, I do, in fact, drink."

"But...whiskey?" She looks at Riggs. "Did you do this to her?"

He holds his hands up. "Hey, Seven was like this when I met her."

Hazel's eyes soften. "Is that what you went by? Seven?"

I nod, trying to swallow the lump in my throat. When Hazel grabs me into a monster hug, it's harder than ever to keep from tearing up. She releases me, and I blink rapidly. "It's what I still go by when I'm here. Only now, everyone knows."

"Well, I love it. And I love you."

"I love you, too," I rasp. "We all miss you."

A shadow crosses her face in the dim light, and there's no mistaking the dip her aura takes. When she doesn't respond, I raise my glass. "To sisters."

She brightens and gets the rest of the sisters' attention. "To sisters," we all say, then clink glasses and sip.

"Please tell me you're up first," Clementine says. "My back and hips are killing me."

"You look adorable," Jasmine says.

"The cutest little sprite on the planet," Juniper coos, then laughs and easily avoids the punch that Clementine throws at her.

Carol gets the crowd's attention, and instead of kicking it off herself, she calls me up.

My family claps as I grip Riggs's hand for support. "Go get 'em, tiger," he murmurs, giving me a kiss on the cheek.

Blowing out a breath, I make my way to the front and take the mic from Carol. "This is for my family." And as Sister Sledge's "We Are Family" starts, I scan the audience. This isn't a hard song, not by a long shot, but it means so much. To have them all here, with Riggs supporting me as always, it's...well, it's everything.

The last month has been full of revelations, one after the other, and I understand that I'm at the very beginning of my journey. And as I begin to sing about having all my sisters with me, the joy that pours into me is almost too much to bear.

And then they all come up. Every sister, plus my mom, climbs onto the small riser and sings with me. A laugh escapes me as I keep going, because holy cow, Jasmine can *not* sing, and she's the loudest, but it doesn't matter. Because we're all singing, our arms around each other, as Riggs and Quinton watch with big smiles on their faces. Behind them, Ava and her boyfriend enter the bar, along with Mrs. Hayes, Mr. Dander, and Coach. And I swear, the whole place is alight in yellow hues of joy, because I'm so full of happiness and love I might burst.

When the song ends, the audience claps as we all hug. Aspen holds on the longest, and as she pulls away, she cups my face. "I'm so fucking proud of you, Mags."

Oof. My heart. I manage a watery smile as she steps off

the riser, and then I compose myself. "Riggs," I gesture him onto the riser, then look at Carol.

He hops up without hesitation and takes the extra mic I hand him, then busts into laughter as Beyoncé's "Crazy in Love" comes on. He barely misses the intro, jumping in on Jay-Z's lyrics and pumping his arms to get the crowd going.

I drop my hips and do my best to channel Queen Bey—there's only so much this white girl can do, let's be real—but I can sing the hell out of this song. Also, I might have practiced a little.

A lot. I practiced a lot.

But I got this. For Riggs. For me. And I give Riggs every bit of my attention as I sing about how someone's love can do what no one else's can.

His eyes are sparkling, partly with love and partly with amusement, because he knows, he *knows*, that even though this is my way of showing him how much I love him, it's also me challenging him to bring it with Jay-Z's part.

And he does. The man doesn't even look at the monitor as he drops into the flow. And when he gets to the part about his texture being the best fur, he smooths his hand over his hair and pulls some kind of Elvis move that has the whole place howling.

God, I love him. So much.

It's no hardship to sing the next part about being sprung. We sing the rest of the song, Riggs joining in to sing the chorus while I make a vocal run up and down, making the crowd cheer. And it's such a gift, all of it. To be up here with him, singing for my family, knowing that I'm right where I'm supposed to be. Finally.

When it's over, and we're both breathing hard and grinning like absolute idiots beneath the multi-colored lights, Riggs pulls me in for a kiss. And it's perfect.

COMING NEXT IN THE SACRED RIVER SERIES:
FAKE DATING FENNEC O'FALLON

The postcard arrives with a return address of Amsterdam, and the date from more than a month ago. On the front is a picturesque photo of a green windmill set against an idyllic stream, and there, gracing the back in purple glitter pen, of all things, is the instantly-recognizable handwriting of Fennec O'Fallon. I'd recognize it anywhere at this point, glitter pen or not.

I turn to the world map next to the card catalog and find The Netherlands on it. After a moment's consideration, I twirl my finger in the air and point at the country. The map fills in with the same purple glitter shade of as the writing on the postcard.

I look back at his words.

> A.,
> Would you believe that Manhattan smells more like weed these days than Amsterdam? I —
> F.

The desire to know what's beneath the swirls of purple pen after that first sentence—the burning *need* to read what he wrote, then scratched out—might be the death of me. I hate not knowing things, and Fennec is well aware of that tidy little fact. He probably laughed as he wrote gibberish and then crossed it out, imagining me muttering a spell to make the words reveal themselves and getting nothing.

"Another letter from your pen pal?"

I nearly leap out of my skin as I turn to scowl at my sister. "Was that really necessary?"

Willow smirks on the other side of the counter and performs a dead-on imitation of what I must have looked like mere seconds ago. "You look like you're trying to decipher one of the world's greatest mysteries."

Pretty sure I was. Fennec O'Fallon has been a mystery to me since we met in a chat room as teenagers, and I don't see that changing any time soon. I shrug, folding the postcard and tucking it into my back pocket. "His handwriting is terrible."

My sister considers me, humming thoughtfully, before pushing a thick, cream envelope toward me. "You forgot this in the mailbox."

I didn't forget it. I *avoided* it. There's a difference.

"Oh?" I do my best to affect an air of nonchalance. As though the envelope doesn't have the power to upend my entire life.

"Don't give me that crap. You know what it is, and I'd bet a dose of Truth Tea that you saw it and left it there." Willow raises her eyebrows and tilts her head, entirely too pleased with herself for figuring me out.

"You should have left it there."

"And miss out on torturing you with one of the few things that gets under your skin? Absolutely not." She grins and rubs her palms together in a poor imitation of an evil genius.

I ignore her *and* the envelope and open the cash register, waving my fingers over the till and using my magic to count the money. It's faster and more accurate, and unlike some of the witches in this family, I use magic every chance I get.

"Where is he now?" Willow asks, changing the subject.

Look at that. She *is* smarter than she looks. "Fennec?"

Willow snorts. "No, the *other* world-famous musician who's your pen pal."

"I don't know. This is from over a month ago."

She grabs the postcard, sliding it across the smooth wood before I have a chance to snatch it and shove it into my pocket. Like me, she inspects it closely, spending almost the same amount of time staring at the ink blot. "What do you think he wrote there, before changing his mind?" she murmurs.

My skin prickles. Annoyed, I snap my fingers and send the postcard flying out of her hand and into mine. "Nothing."

It's always nothing.

Willow makes sure to point the invitation out to Mom when she arrives later that afternoon, loaded down with supplies for the shop from her week-long trip to New Orleans. It's still lying next to the cash register, taunting me every time I ring a customer up. I can't bring myself to touch it. Once I do, it's an acknowledgment that I've seen it, and they'll expect a response.

I am nowhere near ready.

Mom knows better than to handle the envelope. Instead, she looks from the intricate golden calligraphy to me. "Are you going?"

"Don't see that I have much choice."

"You always have choices, Aspen."

I hate it when she goes all motherly on me. As if we haven't practically grown up together, given that she's only twenty years older than my forty-three years. "Not about this, I don't."

Her expression softens. "You know I'd go for you if I could."

"I know," I sigh. She would, too, but she can't. It's the First Daughters Ball, something a firstborn witch is invited to only upon turning forty. I've avoided going for three years. The whispers about my absence are unavoidable, even here in Sacred River, and we're approaching gossip levels of the Ton in one of Jasmine's historical romance books. Not that I've read them.

Lies.

I've read all of them. Not that anyone knows that—it'd ruin my reputation, and I quite enjoy my place as the black cat of the family. Not a literal one, of course; we're not shifters and Uncle Fester is our actual black cat, whenever he deigns to grace us with his presence.

"Calliope went, you know," Mom says.

I raise my eyebrows. "And?"

"And she managed it all just fine."

"Expectations were different then."

Mom laughs, the sound like little bells. "They most certainly were not. She went in the 1980s, not in some prehistoric time. Why do you think *I'm* the one who's still here, in Sacred River, when the rest of my sisters aren't?"

She doesn't get it. Doesn't understand the pressure. Mom is the seventh daughter, and that's a far different situation than being the first daughter. Honestly, I'm not sure how Calliope managed to avoid the responsibilities of it all. "It's still different," I insist.

"If you say so," Mom says, shrugging and moving past it like she always does. She tilts her head toward the counter. "Should I throw it away?"

I stare at the invitation, willing it to give up its secrets.

Maybe I'd feel differently if I knew where it was going to be—there's a big difference in flying halfway across the world versus somewhere in the contiguous United States.

Okay…I'm lying again. I'd give anything to get out of here, even if it was just for a little while. But too many people depend on me, and the shop would probably go under in a week flat if I weren't here to keep Mom focused and Willow on track.

Willow snorts a laugh. "You know it's spelled, Aspen. You're the only one who can open it, and it won't reveal squat until you do."

I barely repress a scowl, and it makes my sister laugh even harder.

"Two weeks," she sing-songs, plucking up the envelope and waving it at me.

Two weeks.

Two weeks to decide which way the rest of my life is going.

Want more? Be sure to sign up for my newsletter to stay up to date on all the latest updates, including when this comes out!

Acknowledgments

Thank you, as always, to my husband. The chef, the maker of ridiculous dad jokes, the steady in the whirlwind of this wild life. I love you.

To my daughter and son: you two are the best. Period.

I'm lucky to be surrounded by an incredibly supportive family, so to my sister, brothers, moms and dads: thank you. Your unwavering support and pride means the world to me.

To my fellow indie authors: without you, I am not sure I'd survive the insanity that is #IndieAuthorLife. Your insight, cheers, and teamwork mean the world to me.

To you, my readers: THANK YOU. I am so grateful for you. You are why I get to do this, and I wake up every day excited to write for you.

About the Author

 Valerie Pepper is an incurable optimist and a firm believer in the girl getting the guy, or the guy getting the girl, or the girl getting the girl, or the guy getting the guy, or basically any way it needs to happen to make a real-life happily ever after, even if it takes more than one try.

When she's not writing, you can find her reading, walking, listening to whatever music suits her mood, and hanging out with her family. She's fascinated with the idea of a capsule wardrobe, but loves clothes and shoes and boots far too much to make a real go of it.

She's currently living out her own happily ever after in Birmingham, Alabama, with her family and maaaaaybe too many shoes. Learn more at www.authorvaleriepepper.com.

Also by Valerie Pepper

Guided to Love Series

The Mechanic's Guide to Getting the Boss's Daughter (*series starter novella*)

The Widow's Guide to Second Chances (Book 1)

The Barista's Guide to The Perfect Steam (Book 2)

The Grump's Guide to Chaos (Book 3)

Sacred River Series

Love Potion No. 69 (*Series starter novella, Book 1*)

Karaoke Chemistry (Book 2)

Fake Dating Fennec O'Fallon (Book 3, coming Fall 2024)

Novellas

Naughty All The Way (November 2023) - Part of the Twelve Days of Smutmas limited-time collection

To Have and To Scold in the *Holidays & Hook-Ups* anthology by The New Romance Cafe (June 2023 - limited edition)